The stories and characters are fictional and any resemblance to real people is strictly intentional. Anyone who is offended probably remembers their part all too well!

ISBN 978-1-4477-5059-8

mixed bag

diane lanoue

This is some fucked-up repugnant shit –
Pulp Fiction

contents

Nikki remembers.

Nikki remembers sitting in a small L-shaped room shrouded in smoke, watching the junkies pace back and forth. She remembers feeling the weird mix of dread and hope; needing the money but not wanting the work.

Doing the intro's (cattle call) the mix of feelings made her seem shy. But that didn't stop her being picked – older business men and Asians mostly. The ones who turned out to be ok when she said she didn't do a full service or oral. The ones who said ok when she offered a topless hand relief instead. Nikki never saw the point in fucking someone for a 100 bucks when you could get 80 just to pull him off.

She once saw a girl who was really hanging out do a lot more for a lot less. She was sweating and shaking, her voice frantic and pleading as she worked feverishly over his cock. The 'sweet' talk took on a grotesque flavour as she pulled and prodded him, hanging for her fix and desperate for the 20 bucks that would only come when he did. This same girl was heroin skinny and kind of sexy but tattooed all over her body. She dressed in full leathers and rode 50km to work on a Harley each day. She ducked out at lunch time to score and smoked pot in the toilet to take the edge off when there wasn't money to get her hit. She would kiss all the girls when she was stoned and threaten them when she wasn't, especially the ones who were getting work or who were younger and cuter than her.

At the time, Nikki never really thought much about which girls were on the shit and which weren't - it actually never occurred to her. Nikki really was naïve about these things – she had never known people who used more than pot. Now she remembers one girl who slept on the couch all day long, stretching slowly and sensuously like a cat when she had to go do a booking. She never seemed to be hanging out – permanently stoned and pretty happy about it. Most of the other girls alternated between happy and sad; manic and sedated; pinned and dilated.

Nikki remembers going home one day and finding a used syringe in her bag and she knew exactly who would have put it there. Another warning; just like the veiled threats from the desperate in the girl's room. The next day the receptionist just shrugged and told her to be more careful with her stuff and to watch who she made friends with.

Nikki took offence at this – she wasn't making friends with any junkies! She only remembers making one real friend there the whole time, admiring her politics and liking her personality.

8

This was a smart, sassy chick with feminist principles and a kick ass attitude. Nikki was amazed that a chick like that would do this job. Nikki was amazed that a chick like that would even give her the time of day.

Nikki was even more amazed that this chick didn't get sacked sooner for telling men to fuck off and storming out of bookings if the guy was a pig or got too grabby.

Nikki was genuinely sad when this girl did finally get sacked – she felt that she had lost the one person she could relate to in this crazy industry. She felt that she had lost the one person that also had self respect and placed value on her boundaries.

Since no-one had actually told her what she should or shouldn't let the men do in the rooms, Nikki didn't let them touch her at all once she learned that she could get away with it. Whenever Nikki got a 2 girl booking and the guy wanted sex, she would stand back and watch while the other girl did the deed. She still took her half of the money though. Nikki always wondered if the guy thought that was how it would go and if his fantasy was ruined forever. A bitter, cynical part of her was glad that she could ruin the fantasy of a man who would come to a place like this.

Even with a topless or a body slide, Nikki didn't let them touch her. Talk in the girls rooms revealed that most girls let them feel their tits and finger them – some did more. Nikki thought this was gross and unnecessary. But some of the girls were even more uptight than she was; Nikki remembers one older girl who came to work dressed in a prim suit (just like Jackie O) and who did her hand jobs wearing latex gloves. Nikki did a 2 girl with her once and the sight of her snapping on surgical gloves and looking so proper was hilarious. She had a cut glass English accent and Nikki remembers her saying 'oh, is that all?' to a guy who came really fast and having to turn away quick so he wouldn't see her laugh. This girl was really quite strange.

In fact, most of the girls were a little strange - she remembers one girl who was about to get married and who was trying to earn some money for the honeymoon (with the groom's blessing). She had fake tits that were like concrete – they looked great but were like hard round balls to the touch. 'Only cost $6000!' She'd say proudly and offer a feel to all the girls. She was very popular with the customers – she had a ballsy attitude and no boundaries. On the other end of the spectrum, Nikki also remembers a very young girl (maybe not even legal yet) who brought a baby lamb into the staff room one day. She said she had found it on the way to work. She wrapped it in a towel and fed it with a bottle. She cried her heart out when the receptionist told her it had to go and called the ranger. Nikki didn't know what a soft girl like her was doing in a place like that or what she needed this dirty money for.

Nikki remembers that most of the girls liked to say they were saving their money for houses. Nikki suspected that most were just saving for their next hit. Most of them had kids. Most of them had boyfriends (some had girlfriends). Some drove flashy cars, some walked and some came in taxi's. She remembers getting taxi's to work when her own car broke down - same driver usually. Sometimes she had a bad day and didn't make enough to pay the fare home. Other days she left with hundreds of dollars; tipping the driver to make up for the days he had let her ride free. She actually went out on a date with that taxi driver once – a fancy dinner and drinks but didn't even kiss him goodnight afterwards. Not really her type after all. He told her that a bloke could get a good full service at one of the cheaper places in town - $17 for 10 mins. She always wondered how he knew that. It turned her stomach to think of fucking someone for 17 bucks. It turned her stomach to think of a guy being happy he had been able to fuck someone for 17 bucks. Nikki believed in fair pay for fair service and could never respect a man who tried to rip a woman off for sex.

Nikki remembers finally getting sick of that place and trying another. She only worked one shift there - no intros, no cattle call. Everyone took turns and she only got one job for the day – 60 bucks. After paying the taxi it wasn't even worth coming in. The other girls were old and tired and made spiteful comments about her dress. She got a migraine with the endless chain smoking and the relentless talk shows blaring in the background.

So she went back to the other place.

Nikki remembers the amazing transformations that took place at shift change. She thinks about the young nurse who turned up crisp and neat in her whites and then put on a long wig and sparkly dress and became a Swedish student trying to earn some money for Uni. Nikki remembers that everyone liked to say they were a student. The clients loved that. Maybe it made them feel less like they were taking advantage, less like admitting that most of the women were putting everything they earned into their arms.

Nikki can't remember the name she used when she tried the next place – she only stayed there for a couple of shifts. She quickly worked out that this was one of the last stops for girls who couldn't get work anywhere else. Most were skinny and sick; on the nod or strung out in the girls room with boyfriends and dealers coming and going, dropping off the gear. There was never many clients there either. The ones that did come in were seedy and sleazy and didn't have much money. But they all still wanted to fuck a supermodel for less than 50 bucks. Nikki would say that she wouldn't even take her clothes off for 50, scraping them up to 70 for a topless hand job. Plenty didn't like her attitude and walked out of the booking to go with someone else. That was fine with her – she had no habit to support so she could afford to turn down the money.

Nikki remembers turning down 200 bucks to fuck an old man who looked like the captain from Gilligan's Island. Later she heard that he told the girl he went with that she looked like his young niece – while he was fucking her. She also remembers another girl telling her how a client kept talking about his 9 year old daughter and her friends in their bikinis – while he was fucking her. It seemed that a lot of men had kid fantasies and wanted to share them. Nikki did not want to know about that sick shit.

So Nikki went back to the other place – at least the clients had money and the receptionists kept out most of the losers and freaks.

Nikki remembers the sailors coming in to port, dreading seeing any of them because they all wanted a full service and were hard to talk into taking less. The other girls loved the sailors because they had lots of cash and were as horny as hell. Because Nikki didn't fuck or suck, she never made much from them. Plus they were all young – Nikki didn't like the young ones – it made her feel like it was more real or something. Nikki remembers one of the girls coming back from a job sobbing, saying that she had told a sailor she would do a body-slide but that when he had asked to massage her and climbed on top, he had raped her. She said that afterwards he acted like it was all ok and offered her his phone number. She said the worst thing was he didn't even pay her for a full service. Nikki thought this was strange.

Nikki remembers that a lot of the clients were a little strange. She remembers a guy who owned a furniture shop trying to talk her into having sex with him, offering to give her a lounge suite if she did. Nikki remembers another guy offering to take glamour photos of her, showing her his portfolio. And another, telling her he loved her - this guy came in about ten times and paid to see her each time but never wanted anything but to talk and ask her to be his girlfriend. Nikki got freaked out and had to get the receptionist to tell him she had quit so he would stop coming in.

Nikki can remember lots of specific incidents and lots of girls and lots of men but Nikki cant remember how over a year went past doing this job that was only meant to be a quick few bucks.

Nikki can't remember how she kept it a secret from everyone, even her boyfriend.

Nikki can't even remember how it all started or how to make it stop.

At first it seemed ok but towards the end Nikki remembers coming home at the end of each week; totally burnt out and barely able to function. Laying in the bath thinking about killing herself then smoking some pot to take the edge off. Then smoking more and more until she didn't even know where the edges were.

Nikki remembers asking herself why she kept going back, but she couldn't find the answer, only that the bills needed paying and maybe she didn't deserve any better.

Nikki remembers one day shaving her head, thinking that surely she'd be sacked or have to quit. She turned up at work in a baseball cap and worked a few shifts looking like a skin-head – it wasn't a problem - the men just didn't care. Turns out they weren't looking at her head anyway.

Nikki remembers feeling tired and old and used up. She took to looking into all the faces of the men she saw in the street, wondering if they had seen her naked. Nikki looked at their wives too and thought – you poor bitches – if only you knew!

Nikki remembers thinking that she would never trust any man.

Nikki remembers thinking she couldn't even trust herself.

Nikki remembers finally deciding to quit and then actually doing it.

Baby's got a bad, bad name.

The beleaguered clerk on the desk at the registry of Births, Deaths and Marriages considered herself somewhat of an expert on names. She knew at a glance what a good name was and especially what a stupid name was. She was an expert not only because she saw thousands of names every year, but because she was the victim of a rather unfortunate name herself. For some unknown reason, her parents had thought it a good idea to name her and her siblings after such far flung places as Paris; Alaska; Cairo; and Tuscany (her 4 sisters). Places her parents had never been and never would. They didn't stop there – she also had brothers named Tennessee and Washington and her own sad moniker was Miami. At least her poor, sad parents had some hope of maybe going to these places one day.

Miami suffered many years of teasing and embarrassment so was determined that when she had children, she would give them solid, strong and most important of all, normal names. She ended up naming her son John and her daughter Mary and warned them to never ever call their own kids anything other than ordinary names. She had thought that this had put paid to the bizarre names once and for all. But now that her family was grown up and she was back in the workforce, it was somewhat ironic that Miami found herself again surrounded by unusual names. Working in this job she came face to face with weird and wonderful concoctions all day long. When she first started at the BDM, she was continually shocked and dumbfounded by the names that people could choose for their offspring. Now years on, she felt she had seen it all and was simply resigned to the stupidity of most people.

Miami was especially disgusted with the young girls - some barely out of puberty themselves, never a man to be seen with them and their wailing litter. These white trash teenyboppers thought it was a great idea to name their kids like ghetto rappers or after the guests on Jerry Springer. She had seen such gems as: Keyshawn; Montell; Teniqua; Waylene; Charnte and Tariq. These were bad, but to her mind, the worst of these types of names were the 'sha' names – names you could hardly pronounce and which the poor illiterate kids themselves would never be able to spell: Lamneisha; Myeesha; Gweneisha; Laquisha; Tamiesha; Kaesha; Niquisha and Tarnarsha.

Miami squirmed every time one of these gum chewing, hipster wearing young mamas came in dragging their latest bundle of joy. She longed to reach a mothers hand over the counter and slap some sense into those empty heads, but she never did. She contented herself with sighing heavily and rolling her eyes as she signed off on these disasters. She only wished she had a rubber stamp that she could use to stamp 'stupid ass name' across their birth certificates and maybe on the mothers foreheads as well.

As irritating as she found the young ones, there were others that were higher on Miami's shit list. Miami had grown up poor in a family that often went without - she knew the importance of a days work and had often been told that money didn't grow on trees. This meant that she found the proudly unemployed hippy parents particularly offensive. They would come in shrouded in a cloud of incense and pot smoke – dressed in tie dyed rags and no shoes, dragging a pile of rag-tag kids with them. Miami just knew that they were the type that had never done a days work and that her tax dollars were supporting these tree-huggers as they churned out tribes of children with embarrassing names. She seethed as she ticked off the new breed of love children: Karizma; Summerstar, Harmony, Jurnee, Raven, Forrest, Gypsy, Breeze, Krystal-Angel, and Freedom. She seriously had to stop herself from 'Saying Something' when a smelly, dreadlocked beatnik (with no bra on of course) thrust a pair of squalling twins in her face and announced that they were to be called; Heaven-Leigh and Heaven-Cent.

As annoying as these grubby parasites were, Miami thought that the well-heeled society types were just a little worse. With their aerobicised bodies and designer tracksuits, they had designer attitudes to match. They would strut in with their impeccably groomed progeny (always 3 or 4 of them) who were invariably dressed in designer childrens-wear and saddled with stupid try-hard names. These types would always introduce each child and Miami would struggle to keep a straight face as they pointed out: Ripley; Keaton; Tanner; Rastus; Chadwick; Taevis; Rainer; Lanndon; Mackenzie; Tallis; and worst of all, a plump little girl ridiculously named Lu-lu-blu.

The yummy mummy would imperiously thrust over the forms for the naming of her latest sprog and wait tapping perfectly manicured nails on the counter. Miami couldn't help herself with these ones and often repeated the name out loud with a cheery and sarcastic, 'Well isn't that a unique name!' By unique, of course she meant pretentious and downright wanky. The yummy mummy would usually smile condescendingly and wheel her perfect family out, smug in the knowledge that they were just a little better than everyone else.

Miami was also bewildered by the mostly normal looking parents that just wanted something a 'little different'. By this they meant ordinary names that had been mangled until they were impossible to spell or pronounce. Miami saw Jaycen; Rocksanne; Khylii; May'C; T'Neil; Genell; Zakriyaa; Emajen; and strangest of all a couple that named their sons Keiff and Seff. Miami was unsure whether they were trying to say and spell Keith and Seth but was assured vehemently that they wanted their sons to be 'special'. Miami guaranteed them that there was no doubt that they would be 'special' with names like that!

The other category of normal looking (but profoundly weird) parents were those that liked to give their children 'stripper names'. Miami was simply confused by names like; Mysteeque; Coco; Tixi; and Slade. The worst of this bunch also mangled the spelling just for a touch of extra class. Miami was horrified when one such mother announced her newborn's name as; Desty'nhh (pronounced Destiny) and stated that she had tried to find something to 'match' her other daughter; Dezeray (pronounced Desiree). Miami was unsure why a person would 'match' children as if they were socks and why a person would want her sweet little girls labelled with pole dancers' names. She cringed every time she had to sign off on one of these.

Miami was also deeply concerned by the strange individuals that deemed it necessary to brand their kids with titles representing their favourite items or characters. These were always intense, brooding types that slouched in and furtively shoved the papers over the counter. She supposed they had reason to be secretive when choosing such titles as; Atari; Lucifer; Taquila; Elvis; Obi-wan; Harlee; Atticus; Lancelot; and Denim. At the opposite end of the spectrum but still deeply concerning were the car name types - some went for the more luxury autos like; Mercedes; Porsche and Cherokee and some went for the standard models; Chevy; Capri; Astra; Caprice; and one memorable Falcon-Ford. Miami usually just stared at these people with one eyebrow cocked.

Because of Miami's sensitivity to the ridiculous, her friends kept an ear out for the bizarre and also attempted to placate her where possible. After a tour of Europe, Miami's friend Nina had told her that in Germany there were restrictions on what a person could name their child and that these names were contained in a book at their BDM. People had to ensure that the name that they wanted was approved and that it was listed in the book – if it wasn't, they couldn't have it. Miami didn't know if this was true but she wholeheartedly agreed with the idea. A few weeks after Nina told her that, just for fun, she drew up her own book of acceptable names and kept it under her desk. She would put a little tick next to each name when someone actually chose one that she approved of and made an entry in another little book when it was one she did not approve of. She had to admit that the book of unacceptable names was much longer and that she rarely had occasion to tick her list.

Miami contented herself with doing this for a few months but the fact that the unacceptable list had filled one little book and was halfway through another drove her to distraction. Then Miami had a brainwave! Instead of just passively accepting the stupidity that these parents were inflicting on their children and society – Miami would do something about it! She began to collect the applications for birth registration and naming that came in. She separated the ones with asinine names and instead of entering them in the database and issuing birth certificates like she was supposed to, she took them home each night and carefully altered them. She then took the altered applications back to the office and issued birth certificates that had normal, sane names on them. She changed them so that instead of reading Tayshaun, it said

Thomas; instead of Paprika it said Penelope; instead of Amber-light it said Anne; instead of Cinderella it said Cynthia; instead of Tallen it said Timothy; instead of Maddicyn it said Michelle; instead of Wyatt it said William. All up, she altered 174 applications over a period of 2 weeks.

Miami then sent the newly corrected birth certificates out to the families and sat back to await the storm that would surely come when they discovered that their attempts to brand their offspring with hideous, ridiculous and grammatically incorrect names had been thwarted. Miami knew that it would be extremely difficult for the disgruntled parents to change these birth certificates back – it would require a whole new application along with the associated fees and deed poll process. Of course Miami intended to deny doing any alteration at all and being a longstanding model employee, she expected that she would be believed. If not, she had typed up a resignation letter and booked a ticket to Germany. She expected that she would fit in a lot better working with their system anyway.

The elevator.

I spent 37 years manning the elevator at Chester House. 8am til 6pm, up and down all day long – took over from my own daddy who ran the elevator for years before me. Chester House is a real old building, smack bang in the heart of the city – it squats gracefully next to shiny silver skyscrapers and modern office towers – one of the few remaining heritage buildings left. A real grand old dame.

Of course she'd been restored and refurbished but the facade remained, including the old elevators. They were the old metal cage type with heavy wrought iron doors that had to be cranked and closed by hand and a wide gap about 15cm across between the landing and the floor of the elevator. They used to be the old manual type that needed an operator to send her up and down, but then they had her fitted with fancy modern machinery that allowed her to run on her own at high speed and open and shut the heavy doors all on her own. I guess my job there was all but obsolete but management still liked the look of a man in uniform to ride inside by the doors, press the buttons and greet the people – gives a touch of class to the place. Plus it was my job to say 'mind your step' whenever someone entered because they never did figure out how to fix the gap without ruining the look of the elevator.

The very last day I worked the elevator was in fact the last day that old thing made the journey up – they fully replaced her after that, with a shiny steel contraption, fully closed in and modern with no gap and no driver at all.

Looking back at what happened that day, I still can't believe no-one tried to help; no-one said anything; no-one moved or screamed; no-one panicked; no-one did anything much at all! We just stood there, staring in disbelief. It could have been one of those group apathy things that the shrink talked about afterwards or maybe some other fandangled traumatic stress condition. But I think it was simpler, more basic than that. I think we just plain couldn't believe our eyes!

What happened was; the fellow had run for the elevator and caught it at the last moment, just as the doors were closing. He had shoved his arm and head through the doors and grinned at us inside – I remember he shouted 'yeah baby' to the other guys from the firm upstairs who were already inside. They all looked the same, with their gelled back hair and expensive suits – rich boys who had been to private school together and now worked together. They had the slick look of the young urban professional – a look that says money not manners – boys who played fast and partied hard. Boys who always got what they wanted and never paid the bill.

His buddies in the elevator clapped and cheered – the other 5 of us just watched in silence – used to the antics and not amused or part of the clique. I stood as usual, stiff and formal to the left of the doors next to the control panel – my face carefully poised and neutral.

The fellow had wedged his head, arm and shoulder through the space between the doors with his other arm and lower body outside as he tried to pull the doors open without dropping his designer briefcase, skinny latte or the keys to his Porsche.

I know you're thinking that when any object is between the doors of an elevator; the doors automatically re-open. And that's true normally – they make them like that now – it's a safety feature. But being that this was an old elevator with real heavy iron doors, they hadn't been able to include this feature in the upgrade, and so the doors didn't re-open. In fact it looked like the doors closed up snug, trapping him by the face, shoulder and arm. He started to panic then – you could see his eyes rolling back. I think he knew that the old girl would start to move and when she did, would shoot express to the 5th floor like she did every morning.

Now I don't know if you have ever given much thought to how much space there actually is between the closed doors of an elevator and the shaft that it runs up, but I've had occasion to think about it quite a bit now and I reckon it couldn't be more than 25-30cm. And that's not taking into account where it stops at each floor and the landing juts out a little into the shaft – the gap there is only 15cm or so.

I don't know if he actually thought about any of that right then but he must have known that he was in some serious trouble because he started to squawk and squeal and his arm flailed about like a mad thing. Right then he must have let go of the coffee, keys and briefcase because his other arm began to beat wildly on the doors.

His face was too compressed for his jaws to open properly so no real words came out but I think we got the gist of what he was screaming – I think he wanted us to help him; to push the emergency button or pry the doors open – or just do something! Of course, none of us did that – otherwise things might have turned out differently – we all just stood there, dumbstruck and disbelieving as the elevator started to move.

Now, you understand that although she still had the old character look to her, inside her was 'state of the art' new and improved machinery just like the new elevators now. They are designed to move important people quickly between floors. They take off fast and get where they're going fast.

I ask myself every day how things might have been different if she hadn't been re-done and was still the old hand cranked kind. Of course I also ask myself everyday how things would have been different if I had had the presence of mind to stop her before things got bad. The sight and sound was bad enough on the day, but it seems to get worse the more I replay it in my mind.

I don't think there is anything to quite compare to the sound of human flesh tearing and bones snapping. The sound of the fellow's spine cracking in two as it hit the first landing was horrifying – and it really doesn't pay to spend too much time thinking about just how a human body fits through such a small space. Lord knows I can't help but dwell on it and my mind keeps picturing him, like a sausage hit in the middle with a hammer – meaty blood and guts spurting from both ends.

His mangled body made it past the first landing and I swear I could hear the skin ripping off in shreds as his shattered back and legs were dragged up the inside wall of the elevator shaft. Amazingly he was still alive and conscious even while blood was spraying in through the cage and pouring out of his mouth. His eyes were huge and bulbous in his face which was pinched and scarlet.

The elevator continued its journey and we all stood in silence – mouths open and eyes bulging – none of us said anything or made a sound. The fellow continued to gobble and shriek through a mouthful of blood as his skin was flayed off his body and his broken bones banged and bashed against the doors and shaft. We were all drenched in the shower of body fluid that rained over us, yet we still stood silent.

The next landing seemed to rip the bottom half of his torso completely off and a huge wave of blood gushed in through the doors. His dangling intestines flapped and swung from his ruined body and landed at the feet of the stunned passengers who glanced down but still didn't make a sound.

God's honest truth, I am still not convinced that he was actually dead, even then. Of course the papers all said that he had died instantly but we all know that wasn't true. It was nowhere near instant. And even then, despite the massive trauma, with half his body ripped clean off, I swear I still saw his mouth working and chest heaving for a few more seconds. The look in his eyes haunts me every day and those glittering orbs stare back at me every night in my dreams.

The fellow finally did stop breathing and making noise and his ravaged torso just hung there, clenched between the doors, oozing blood and goo. The elevator finally slowed and arrived at the 5th floor where the doors opened and what was left of the fellow slipped to the floor with a sickening plop. His eyes were still open and he lay there looking up at us accusingly. Unbelievably, we were still silent and unmoving, frozen in shock despite being heavily spattered by body fluid and flecks of skin.

It was only when a young secretary came out of her office and caught sight of the gore that we seemed to wake up. Her screams rose and fell like the old air raid sirens and soon everybody in the elevator joined her. They howled and wailed as they slipped and stumbled and slid, fighting to get out and

away from the fellow. Even his buddies didn't stick around –
this was obviously not something that their fancy upbringings
and expensive educations had prepared them for.

Only I kept standing there – my hand was poised and frozen,
hovering over the control panel only centimetres away from
the emergency stop button that could have prevented the
whole mess from happening. I must have stood there for near
on half an hour (until the police and ambulance arrived
anyway) and then a real nice lady led me away to drink hot
sugary tea and asked me again and again if I was alright.

I said I was ok and I walked home that night, even though it
was almost 15 blocks. My uniform was sticky and stained with
blood and my hair and face was crusty with it and other body
fluids. A few kind people asked me if I was ok – if I needed
any help – but most just stared at me as I trudged on by. I
finally reached my apartment and fell to the floor. I could only
move once that night and that was to grab a bottle of bourbon.
That bottle didn't leave my hand until I sucked her dry. I fell
asleep on the carpet fully dressed, clutching the empty bottle
and an old teddy bear.

The next day I called up my boss on the telephone and told him I wouldn't be in that day and not to expect me the day after either. In fact I told him I would be retiring early and that I wouldn't be back in at all. Actually, he was real nice about it and ended up couriering my things to me along with a fat cheque. But I never could bank that cheque and I think I vaguely remember burning it in a drunken haze along with my uniform in the fireplace.

I never did go back to Chester House – in fact I even went out of my way not to go anywhere near it ever again. Now all I want is to forget and I still drink every day trying so hard to forget. But I can still see that fellow's face in my mind, clear as day. No matter how much bourbon I put away. And you know, somehow the worst thing is that no-one ever did ask me why I didn't push that little button. No-one ever blamed me or questioned me or even looked at me sideways. Not even the shrink ever once said anything about it. Course I ask myself often enough; mostly late at night when I can't sleep and the bottle is dry and those haunting eyes just stare and stare at me.

Justice.

It was hard to pinpoint exactly when the hurt and anger turned to hate, but when it did, an idea was born. A horrible idea. A fantastic idea. An idea so delicious it had to be considered and planned for and held as close as a talisman to ward off the pain.

After all, how many nights had she spent crying into her pillow or lying awake wondering where he was and who he was with? And how many times had her pride been pushed aside with her dignity, making her taking him back 'just one more time'? And how many times had she looked into his lying eyes and chosen to believe the words that did not sound convincing (even to his own ears)? How many phone calls were promised but did not come? And finally, every time, catching him in the lie. Catching him doing the unspeakable and yet again, not forgiving but choosing to forget.

Truly (she had to admit), this whole mess was not solely his fault, and the only hate greater than the one she felt for him, was for herself. She was so damn weak. So willing to put up with his games, just to avoid being alone. It was not that she was an unattractive girl, because she had once thought herself to be quite becoming. But after all these years with him and his constant cutting criticisms of her hair, her weight, her clothes…she began to look at herself in a much harsher light. She began to say to herself that she was lucky to have him, and besides, weren't all men the same?

Not that he was anything special to look at! And his social skills were somewhat lacking. And truthfully, he was quite selfish in the bedroom. But then again, if he was so ordinary, why did he seem to have no trouble finding willing partners? And why was she so unwilling to let him go? It couldn't have been his money – for although he made a tidy sum each week – he had in fact only bought her two presents in all the time they had been together. Several birthdays, Valentines days and Christmases were bypassed and yet he was forgiven for his thoughtlessness again and again.

It certainly wasn't his warmth or support that she stayed for, with his snide remarks about her work and his patronising tolerance of her hobbies. He never missed a chance to belittle the bronzed knick knacks that she made, even when she sold them successfully at markets and to friends. His continual jibes about her dreams of opening a shop were cruel and his constant criticism of her writing was callous.

So you can see that it was not any specific event that brought her to the conclusion that something must be done. Rather a gradual understanding that something had to be done to teach him a lesson and to free herself while there was still something worth freeing. It was only another lonely night in front of the TV, pondering where he might be. Another night of waiting for his call and even after midnight, keeping the television down low and rushing back from the bathroom in case the phone should ring and she might miss it.

It was this night, of all the similar nights, that a little voice began to speak up inside her head. The voice began to ask her all sorts of questions that hurt to hear and that were surely best left unanswered. This persistent little voice would not be silenced and soon she began to listen to it. It was this night that she finally decided that it was time for her man to try some of his own medicine and see if he liked its bitter, choking taste.

The only thing that gave her pause was deciding how to hurt a person who evidently had no heart and definitely no conscience. And how to hurt him in such a way that he might never again regain his cocky arrogance and strutting-two-faced ability to gain trust again and again. For it would be true to say that she didn't know of any one thing that he cared enough about to worry about losing. Certainly not her. Even going so far as to think about killing him didn't seem like enough payback for all the years of hurt. It wasn't enough to compensate for all the time that he had kept her prisoner with his sly charm. It wasn't enough to make up for whatever it was that kept her clinging to the hope that one day he would change into Mr Right.

It was this analogy of him keeping her prisoner that finally gave her the idea. The idea that had her clenching her eyes shut in delight, dreaming of how perfect it would be to have him as her prisoner. How perfectly just. For really, all he had ever valued was his freedom. His ability to go where he wanted with whom he wanted, regardless of the people hurt by his infidelities.

It was this night that she began to seriously consider the possibilities and problems involved with actually keeping him as a captive in her home. It would have to be a proper prison, with the right amount of deprivation and punishment fitting someone like him. In fact, with a few modifications, the wine cellar below the kitchen would make the perfect place for him to spend the rest of his days.

It was on this very night that she began to draw up plans and make lists of things to buy and build. Things that would fit together to let her take back her life and to make him pay with his.

So this is how it began, the idea that was set to change her from the timid little mouse that she had become back into the queen that she had long desired to be. He would be put in his place, a low and despicable creature, imprisoned at her pleasure. Because honestly, if she was to work it out, he really did owe her at least four years to make up for the four that she had wasted with him. And then there was her responsibility to stop him from using any other girls as she had been used – this would account for the rest of his life being taken from him.

When it was all said and done, plans made and cell finally built, she had to congratulate herself for being able to do this – he had always said she was useless with her hands. He said she must be dim-witted, she had so few skills. She stood back admiring her work; glad to have proven him wrong at last.

As it turned out, it was not that hard to capture him (once he had actually made the time to see her). It was easy to convince him to go to the cellar for a bottle of red, and once he was there, he was hers. She allowed herself a rare smile as the steel door slammed shut on his tiny room, his shocked face almost comical in its surprise.

She had to admit, the room *was* very small- only about 2 metres by three – enough to lie down if he wished and big enough that he wouldn't have to sleep in his own excretement (for a while). She didn't expect him to have much opportunity to sleep anyway, as she planned to keep up a cycle of lights. She had wired these on a timer that would go off and on at random, sometimes after only one or two minutes, sometimes allowing him an uninterrupted half hour of darkness. She had also neglected to furnish the room with any carpet or bedding and the cellar was quite damp and cold, making sleep difficult.

At first she had thought that she wouldn't feed him either but she decided that would be un-necessarily cruel and not worthy of her. Besides, once he was there, she found that it was quite fun to make him special treats – sometimes putting in bugs and cockroaches to surprise him as he ate. Once she presented him with a whole rat, roasted and dressed. She had to admit, he was stubborn - it did take him 4 days of eating nothing at all before he finally gave in and consumed it.

But most fun of all were the videos that she made of herself, feasting on delicious food, having a hot shower, talking to friends (even, maddeningly discussing his mysterious disappearance, which all agreed was very selfish and 'just like him').

Several times she filmed herself making love with his best friend. She presented these videos to him on his 'TV nights' when she would sit down there with him and let him see what he was missing out on. She really felt that this video idea was inspired – now he could know how it felt to be on the outer, watching the action but never part of it!

It was funny though, once he was there, her prisoner, she began to feel less and less for him. Even less hate. He began to be merely another chore. Something that needed food and water and something to tease and torment when she was bored but not an obsession anymore. In fact, it seemed like their roles had reversed because he would spend his nights crying and waiting for her to appear. He would beg her to stay and believed her when she said she would be back soon.

She had to admit, even though he bored her now, she had come to like the feeling of power and ownership over him. She began to see how he must have felt during their relationship. She also came to understand how he must have felt pressured by her, having to make an appearance, having to deal with the constant tears and recriminations. She began to think of ways to get rid of him, to avoid having to deal with him. It played on her mind all the time, the guilt and the responsibility.

It became so much of a burden, so much of a hassle to even walk down there, that she began to leave it for days at a time. She kept waiting for him to express regret over the way that he had treated her, to apologise for his behaviour. She felt that if he would just do this, it would be the catalyst for a discussion between them, the road to healing and to his freedom. But the apology never came – in fact; she had to give him some grudging credit for not once saying sorry for anything. He seemed to have that much pride, or stupidity left.

It began to bother her so much, the dilemma of what to do with him, whether to let him out or not, that she started to avoid going to him at all. Sometimes she left him for more than a week. On the last occasion, it had been nearly three weeks when she had finally decided that he could have his freedom regardless of his refusal to face his faults.

Because she had been thinking so much about what to say and how to say it, she was not prepared to see him there; silent and lifeless in his own waste. Skinny and dirty beyond recognition, his mouth open in an eternal scream, eyes staring blankly. All his power to hurt her was gone, along with his life.

In actual fact, after the initial shock, this made her quite angry! It was so typical of him to avoid confrontation like this! She was bitterly disappointed that he had died before she could set him free and see if he had learned from his mistakes. She had to admit in the face of his death that did shed a tear for what might have been and for the love that had made her teach him this hard lesson. She had to admit too, that she had been looking forward to the moment she would set him free and she had imagined that he would have turned to her and admitted that she had been right. That he still loved her and that they would live happily ever after. It was typical of him that he had avoided taking any responsibility or making a commitment, as he always had.

It was this final lingering annoyance at him that caused her to decide that her last act of punishment would be to ensure that he would be with her forever.

And so it began, the rebuilding of herself that could finally start now that the issue of 'him' was sorted out.

She moved to a new place, leaving everything behind. Everything but the one thing that her new friends and neighbours commented on and wondered over. An 'object d'art'. A life size and life like bronze statue of a man who appeared to be in the throes of an agonising death. A piece that she had painstakingly crafted and now displayed in her sitting room with the other knick knacks and which she titled 'Justice'.

Snapshots

I remember asking him once why he wouldn't stop using.

It's fucking you up, I said

He laughed and said, *no it's fucking you up! You can't deal with it! Why would I want to stop?*

Then I asked him what was so good about it.

He shook his head, a wry grin on his face and spoke in staccato;

that moment before you slide the steel in...

that second of anticipation...

that desire...

that knowledge of whats to come...

then it hits you and floods you with waves of pleasure...

nothing better...

everything is good when you're loaded...

All this said with breathless joy, excitement filling his eye – more enthusiasm than I had seen in him for ages. Then, bitter, with a sigh;

But you wouldn't know about that, would you Miss goody-fucking- two-shoes? You only know what you see on TV – some skinny loser banging up in an alley, selling his ass for the next hit. Well fuck you! You think that's what its all about don't you – you think you know all about it because you've seen it on 'A Current Affair', hay? Well until you step outside your safe little world; until you actually understand what it is that you think is fucking me up – spare me this moralising bullshit…

The last bit was muffled by the belt he held clamped in his teeth. Done mixing up, he had tied the belt while speaking and now, defiantly, looking into my eyes, slid the needle in. The belt fell slack, his eyes rolling back. Conversation over.

This was only one of many conversations we had, way before things got bad. In a way, he was right – he was not by any stretch of the imagination, some skinny loser hanging out in an alley. He was the poet, philosopher, musician, model with movie star looks and a heart of gold. He would be more likely to help an old lady across the street than hit her over the head for cash.

Cash was never a problem for him anyway – he made his money doing photo shoots for magazines and billboards. You might have seen him in Calvin Klein on the freeway or sipping coke on the back of a bus – whatever the product was, the real star was him. He was what the photographers called a phenomenon – he looked great in every shot – no bad angles, no red eyes, no dorky smiles. Even the silly beach and bbq snapshots someone would take over the summer would showcase him, shining out of the group – a work of art.

Because we grew up side by side, I had hundreds of snapshots of us. In the sandpit and wading pool. At home and on holidays. Of us dressed up at Halloween, him sharing his lollies when I got less. Us at my school ball when I couldn't get a date (envy of all the girls with him on my arm!). Us at my 21st, us at his 21st, us at weddings, parties, everywhere. A snapshot of us for every significant event in our lives.

He always thought the whole modelling thing was a big laugh and kept copies of his photos in the same black frames, all over the house. *Shrine to perfect genes,* he would say, but not in a conceited way, just taking the piss. The simple fact was, he knew he was gorgeous – how could he not? But it never became an obsession with him – he knew that his looks were his cash cow and he was always down to earth. He knew that the modelling would pay the way for him to follow his real dreams of writing and playing music. He would write songs and sing, accompanying himself on the keyboard. His long fingers would stroke the keys, his voice haunting as he sang about looking for meaning. He used to say music was the way for him to give a voice to his soul. I would sit beside him as he sang and in the later days, when he would nod off mid song, I would hold him in my arms for hours.

His affair with heroin began in the summer of '98, the summer he turned 23. He had lots of work, lots of cash and lots of opportunities. Most of those models were high pretty much all the time and soon he was joining them. Hitting up at parties, then on jobs, then anywhere and everywhere. At first it was just a fun thing for him, when his habit really was just a habit. Before it became his life.

As it got more of a hold on him, he stopped playing his music, stopped writing and got defensive and evasive about how much he was using. It seemed that the more he used, the more he needed. He sometimes said he had to hit up just to feel normal. Sometimes he would phone me late at night, hanging out, crying, and saying he was going to stop, asking me to help him. The next day he would score again and feeling better, deny he had even called me.

The funny thing about him and the heroin was that he never lost his looks. He never became that typical strung out user – sure he lost weight, but it just gave him a lean, hungry animal appeal that others wanted to imitate. Sure, his pupils were always either pinned or huge black open saucers, but you had to look close to see that. The makeup and lighting covered a lot and no-one really wanted to ask any questions. Even at his worst; hanging out or nodding off, he was stunning. Enough to make you look twice – enough to make you fall in love at first sight.

Was I in love with him? I am not ashamed to say that I was and always will be – loving him not only as my twin brother but in love with the person he was, the magic he had. When things were really bad, he used to scream that I just wanted to 'save' him, that I didn't really care about him. But I know what I felt when I looked into his eyes, when I heard his laughter, when he smiled, when he cried. I felt the same as I did when we were small – as if the world was still perfect, as if our dreams were still possible. Yes, it was love, of the purest kind. And yes, I did want to save him, but only because I wanted him so badly to keep on being the person he always was. And because it was such a waste, what he was doing to himself, what he was doing to me.

We never had the typical sibling relationship – we never fought and always hung out together, we were inseparable. I always looked up to him; he was the one to make me see beauty in life, the good things when I saw only bad. He was always there when I was alone or hurting, he was the one with advice and a shoulder to cry on. He was the one next to me in all the snapshots – brother, protector, supporter, soulmate, friend.

So many snapshots over the years...

But the last snapshot of him was a portrait – special police issue in grainy black and white;

His cold blue body...eyes wide open...needle still in his arm, belt pulled tight.

His beautiful face contorted...tongue swollen...an ugly pool of vomit in a halo around his head.

His arms, legs, feet covered in tracks and dried spots of blood...

Head thrown back...

Dead on the bathroom floor.

Cheatin'

A woman knows.

When her man's heart, his mind, his *dick* is somewhere else.

Of course he will say it ain't true – he will swear on his first born's life that it ain't so. He's lying and she knows it.

Its like that skit Eddie Murphy used to do in the 80's – you can catch your man stepping right out of another woman's bed, pants around his ankles and dick dripping – and he will still say 'it wasn't me'. Then of course when his back is to the wall and he *finally* admits to something; there are the distinctions he will make and the definitions he will try to twist to his advantage. Just like that infamous president who was caught cheating…he'll tell you that oral sex aint sex at all and he wouldn't touch 'that woman' anyhow.

Or if he is forced to admit to something; he'll tell you how it didn't count cuz you were separated; or that it was only business with a gal who gets paid for it; or that it was just a drunken kiss between friends; or that it was "just sex" because you rejected him and that brought up his childhood issues; or that it was a comfort fling with his ex; or a quickie with the neighbour; or just a bit of touchy feely when he had a few too many drinks and pills. Its always "just" because of something you did and its always, *always* your fault.

Then (like Eddie said) when he's finally cornered, he'll try to explain it away. He'll say "yeah, I admit it, I fucked her! Ok, I fucked **her**.....but I *make love* to **you**". And that's supposed to melt your heart and make you forgive him.

The sad thing is, most times it does! We are stupid bitches, us women. We really are! We know they lie and they cheat and they lie some more and still we smile and turn the other cheek (and the other and the other). We screw each others men and we scratch each others faces instead of theirs. We chase after them and we phone them and we drive by their houses. We breed their children, and raise up other women's children - all hoping they'll just love us. We put up with their shit and we let them treat us like shit.

The funny thing is; god forbid if we cheat; then they beat us and they stalk us and sometimes they kill us…and the other guy…and sometimes our kids too. Jerry Springer's made a career out of this crap – and yet we keep on doing it and letting them do it to us.

Well that is – some of us do. Others of us actually wise up and take some action on the situation. Some of us turn the tables and get our revenge.

It still takes years and many nights alone and too many phone numbers found and too much perfume smelled…but eventually, some of us wise up.

My man was a nasty no-good piece of work who liked to cat around on a Saturday night and crawl back into my bed thinking I was none the wiser.

Well, I guess I have to admit, I *was* none the wiser for a good 10 years or so. Then I got plenty wiser and one night I was waiting in that bed with a big ol' butcher knife. I was gonna do him like Lorena Bobbitt did her man but lying there, I got to thinking. I decided I didn't want to spend the rest of my life in jail – that would really defeat the purpose of getting free of this no-count loser. So I slid the butcher knife under my pillow and faked being asleep like I did every other Saturday night and waited for him to stop farting and fussing and fall asleep. Then I slipped out of that bed and into his car, grabbing his wallet along the way. I knew he wouldn't miss any money I'd take – he'd just think he'd drunk it and fucked it away like he normally did.

I drove about 100kms, two towns along and into the city, to the real seedy part where the gals who walk the street look like they'll blow you for 5 dollars and a cigarette. I was looking for a particular type of gal and not any old one would do. I cruised around for the better part of the night until I saw what I was looking for. Blonde and busty. Just like he likes best, but real skinny and kinda sick looking, with a nasty red sore on her neck.

I pulled up slow next to her, wound the window down and called out;

'hey sister'.

She looked in at me and shook her head 'Sorry, I don't do chicks'.

I held out $50 and said 'I just wanna talk to you'.

She looked right and left up the street and peered in at me again, obviously trying to see if I was a cop. I guess my flannel pyjamas convinced her I wasn't because she finally opened the door and slid in to the passenger seat.

'We can't sit here – you better drive' she said, lighting up a smoke.

We drove in silence a while and then she said, 'So what you wanna talk about anyhow?'

I looked over at her and tried a little smile – 'You look kinda sick' I said.

'So?' She spat, 'What – you a doctor?' she cackled with reedy laughter that soon ended in a coughing fit.

'No I aint no doctor that's for sure. You look like you got the AIDS. You all skinny and shit – is that what you got?'

She looked at me, eyes narrowed. 'Look – *you* aint fucking me – what do you care what I got or what I don't got?'

I smiled for real then – 'You're damn right *I* aint fucking you – but I will pay you to fuck someone I know, if you *do* have what I think you got.'

She shook her head, blowing smoke into my face, 'You are one sick bitch. I think I wanna get out now – you can keep your money.'

I looked at her confused - 'Why? Its just a job right? And you look like you need the money – I can see your hands shaking. I'll pay you real well. You can get yourself a hit and a meal – maybe somewhere to sleep for a few nights. Whats wrong with that?'

She looked over at me again, eyes narrowed, 'Yeah I got the AIDS but I work safe. I use a rubber every time, even for head. You think I want to give some guy this shit?'

I smiled wryly at her, 'Didn't some guy give *you* this shit?'

We drove along in silence for a while longer – each of us thinking stuff in our own minds. "Well how much we talking about?' she finally said, 'And how you know he aint gonna call the cops when he find out I got this shit? In fact what makes you think he gonna fuck me anyway when he get a look at me – you knew straight away I had the sickness.'

I laughed out loud then. 'Girl you oughta know a man will fuck anything.'

She smiled over at me and I knew I had her then, 'That's true enough' she said.

We kept on driving around for about another hour while we cooked up the plan – I gave her $100 for her trouble that night and we settled on $1000 for the rest of the job – all she had to do was turn up at his local bar next Saturday night and do her thing. All I had to do was get myself along to the bank and set up a big life insurance policy for my honey and then somehow avoid my wifely duties until his untimely passing.

After;

I'm sure no-one was surprised to hear when he got the AIDS – probably surprised he never got it earlier, what with all the women he's been with. Did me some good in the community too, with everyone feeling sorry for the poor widow and all. Its pretty bad when your man's caught cheating let alone when he brings a sickness home too. Just as soon as I made it clear to everyone that I was clean, I did real well out of all the sympathy. Maybe the men will do well too, to remember what can happen when they don't keep their dicks in their pants.

Dunstan Harper.

Dunstan Harper was *slow*. Everyone knew that. Especially his mother who had tied his shoelaces and wiped his butt for the last two decades and who still had to check under the bed for boogeymen at night. Dunstan Harper had been walking on God's green earth for 24 years, was 6ft tall and weighed in at over 100 kilos - but he was still only about 7 years old in his mind and always would be.

Moira Dunstan had always known that her boy was different from the other children and admittedly, she had coddled him a bit when she finally found out the extent of his disability. This was much to the chagrin of his father Merv who had always believed that a son should be treated hard so he would grow up tough. Merv soon learned that treating Duncan hard only ended in tears and his father had given up on him long ago. Duncan Harper was definitely and wholly a mummy's boy.

Growing up, Duncan didn't play sports or help his dad in the shed – he liked to cook and do the washing with his mummy. He liked to pretend *he* was the mummy. This was fine with Moira Harper, who had always wanted a daughter but was thwarted by the hysterectomy she had to have after Duncan's birth. She taught him to put the dishes away and peel the vegies. Even though he couldn't be trusted alone in the kitchen, she often gave him small responsibilities that were overseen with a watchful eye. Merv often came in and made smart remarks about his burly son wearing an apron - he couldn't believe that his strapping lad was not only soft in the head but a sissy too.

The first time that Moira Harper found a pair of little girl's underpants in her son's room, she had dismissed it and thought nothing of it – perhaps the washing had got mixed up with someone else's at the Laundromat. The second time, she asked Duncan where they had come from and when he, blushing and giggling, told her that they were little Mae's from next door and that she had given them to him while playing 'mummys and daddys', she had actually thought this was kind of sweet. Duncan was always playing with the smaller children from the neighbourhood – his large frame folded up in the cubby house or squashed at the small table having a tea party. After all, he was just a child in a man's body and Moira Harper never thought much of it beyond that.

The day Moira Harper caught her son masturbating, she was initially shocked and horrified. This was her baby boy! Her sweet docile man-child. After frantically rushing him to the doctor, slowly she began to understand that while his mind was forever locked in childhood, his body and hormones had continued to develop. He now had a man's desires and needs with only a child's understanding of what to do with it all. She began to observe him closer when he was with the neighbourhood kids and was relived when she saw little to arouse her suspicions. Moira did notice that most of the other children did not share his apparent obsession with his genitals and often ran squealing and laughing from him if he suggested playing 'doctors and nurses' or 'mummys and daddys'.

One day Moira came upon him and 9 year old Jenny Cross from up the road, in the cubby house. They were both undressed and looking at each other's bodies. Moira wasted no time telling Duncan to get his clothes on and get home. She then sent Jenny Cross packing with a sharp slap to her ear and a warning not to come around any more. Later that night Moira tried her best to explain to Duncan that he could not play with the little girls alone anymore and that it was naughty to get undressed in front of them. Moira told Dunstan that if he wanted to touch his own privates, that he needed to do that in his own room when he was alone.

Moira truly believed that Duncan did understand this and so was completely shocked and totally horrified a few months later when the local police came with Duncan in the back of the paddy wagon. They told her that he had been found at the park, trying to get young girls to come into the bushes with him. Tearfully, Moira assured the officers that this would never happen again and that Duncan would be under constant supervision. At her wits end, Moira allowed Merv to have his way and he gave Duncan a fair walloping with his belt.

After that, Moira began to secretly watch her son day and night. She was not really concerned that he was some kind of sexual pervert but just that it looked so wrong for a grown man to be playing these games with children. Never mind the fact that he was a child in his own mind. She did not want the neighbours to 'talk' or for anyone to think that they had raised him wrong. Moira took Dunstan back to the doctor, who assured her again that all was normal and that he was just a child exploring his body. The doctor, a kindly old gentleman, thought that Moira was a typical neurotic mother and offered her some valium to settle her nerves.

After many weeks of keeping him inside and not seeing anything to alarm her, tentatively she began to let him out to play again. Everything seemed fine and Moira started to relax. She observed Dunstan playing tea parties and ball games with the other children and did not see any more of the 'other' behaviour. She did notice that her son now spent more time alone in his room and seemed to go through more underwear than he had before – she assumed that he was taking her advice and decided not to discuss this with him.

Everything seemed as though it was back to normal, until a few weeks later on a Thursday. Thursday was the day that Moira and Dunstan took their weekly trip to the shops and stopped at the library for story books to bring home. Moira was reading the gossip magazines while Dunstan chose the picture books he wanted – or so she thought. Unknown to her, Dunstan had slipped out of the library and out the public conveniences to the rear of the building. Usually Dunstan would not go to the toilet by himself and Moira was forced to accompany him whenever he felt the urge.

Moira was unaware that anything was amiss until about ½ an hour later when she noticed a frantic woman racing around the library calling "Abbey? Abbey?"

The woman stopped in front of Moira and said, "Excuse me, but have you seen a little girl with blonde pigtails and a red dress? My Abbey is 6 years old and I can't find her!" Moira shook her head and told the woman that she hadn't seen her. The woman bustled off in search of her daughter. Moira looked back down at her magazine but suddenly felt a pang of alarm and unwanted thoughts started to enter her mind. She quickly jumped to her feet and walked to the children's section, where she fully expected to see her son engrossed in the picture books.

He wasn't there! Moira sucked in a shocked breath and started to panic. She raced around the inside of the library looking for Dunstan but he was no-where to be found. Moira went to the help desk and asked the librarian if she had seen Dunstan. The librarian smiled and whispered that Dunstan had taken his little sister to the toilet. Moira's eyes bulged – only she knew that Dunstan didn't have a little sister!

She raced outside to the toilet block – no-one was in the ladies toilets and the disabled cubicle was empty too. Moira steeled herself and went into the men's. One cubicle at the far end was locked and Moira pounded on it until a startled grey haired man peered out. Moira hurriedly apologised and ran from the toilet block. Where could he be? Moira looked all around the gardens and did not see anyone. She raced back in to the library and up to the desk again to see if Dunstan had somehow managed to slip back in without her seeing him. The librarian smiled and pointed over to the children's area where Dunstan sat cross-legged with a little blonde girl on his lap. The girl wore pigtails and a red dress. She looked like she had been crying.

Moira stalked over to them. "Dunstan Harper!" she exclaimed. "Where have you been? You know you don't just go off without me like that!"

Dunstan looked up and smiled at his mother – "My friend Abbey wanted to go to the toilet" he said, "And because I am a big boy, I knew where to take her"

Abbey looked up and a tear rolled down her face. She quickly wiped it away and started to stand up. Dunstan grabbed her arm and whispered something in her ear and then let her go. She quickly ran from the children's area and into her mother's arms, who was pacing frantically by the front desk. Moira eyes followed the little girl and when she turned back to Dunstan she noticed that he was furtively stuffing something into his pocket. "What do you have there Dunstan?" she demanded.

Dunstan looked guiltily at his mother – "Nothing" he mumbled. "Abbey gave me a present". Moira narrowed her eyes at him but decided to leave it – it had been a long day and by now she was flustered and very eager to get home. They gathered their books and made their way out of the library. Moira noticed that Abbey did not return Dustan's smile and wave; she simply shrunk further behind her mother.

Later that night as Moira gathered the dirty clothes, she found nothing in Dustan's pocket – it must have been a lolly or some other little trinket she supposed. Dunstan himself didn't mention anything and was as good as gold that night, eating his dinner and going to bed without a fuss.

Days and weeks went by and nothing happened to give Moira Harper cause to worry. Dunstan played nicely with the children and continued to be mummy's little helper around the house. So when Mrs Fraser phoned to see if Dunstan could come along to her little Crystal's 8th birthday, Moira gladly agreed. Excitedly, Dunstan had chosen a present for Crystal and was up and dressed in his best clothes by 7am on the day of the party. Moira dropped him off at lunchtime with another quick swipe at the cowlick in his hair and a warning to 'be good and do what you are told'. Moira was looking forward to a few hours respite and intended to have a long bath and really relax.

It was 2pm when the phone call came through – a hysterical Mrs Fraser screaming down the line. Moira could hardly understand a word she was saying but gathered that something had happened at the party and she was to come immediately for Dunstan. Moira flung the phone down and raced around the corner, still damp and wrapped only in her robe after her bath. She could see the flashing lights of a police car on the street and worse, an ambulance parked in the driveway. Her heart started to race in fear – had something happened to Dunstan? She picked up her pace and was sprinting by the time she reached the front garden.

A group of crying children huddled near the front door and she could see her Dunstan lying face down on the ground, handcuffed, with a police officer kneeling on his back.

"What's going on?" she screamed, running over to the police officer restraining her son. The officer looked up at her.

"Mam, I'm going to have to ask you to move away from here"

"That's my son you have there" she shouted, "Whats going on?"

The look on the officer's face was enough to let her know that something terrible had happened. She could see Dunstan writhing on the ground and his face, stained with tears peered up at her.

The officer attempted to placate her, "Mrs...?"

"Harper!" she cried hysterically, "Moira Harper! And that there is Dunstan! Now please! Tell me what has happened."

The officer signalled to another uniformed man near by and this policeman took Moira by the arm and led her over to the police car by the kerb. This officer had a pen and pad of paper full of scratchings – she couldn't see what he had been writing.

"Please" she sobbed, "Please tell me what Dunstan has done – why is he being held down like that?"

The officer cleared his throat and said, "Mrs Harper, there has been a terrible incident and to the best of our knowledge at this time, your son is the perpetrator."

"Dunstan wouldn't hurt anyone!" She cried. "He's not *all there* if you know what I mean."

"Yes mam, we did notice that he seemed a little... *slow*... but that doesn't change things – a little girl has been hurt and by all accounts, your son is the one who hurt her."

Just then, Moira saw two ambulance officers wheeling a stretcher down the driveway. She could see a small hump under a white sheet, but the face of the person was completely covered. Moira had watched enough TV to know that this meant that the person on the stretcher was dead. She moaned out loud and sunk to the ground, sobbing.

A weeping Mrs Fraser followed the stretcher down the drive. She spotted Moira Harper crumpled on the ground and flew up to her. She was incoherent and screeching in her rage and grief. It was this picture that the newspapers ran on the front page the next day – Moira crying on the ground and Helen Fraser looming over her – both of them with hair wild and tears staining their faces.

"Your son is a monster" she shrieked "He killed my baby"

Moira struggled to her feet and reached out her hand to Helen Fraser, "My boy isn't violent," she said "This is all a mistake"

Mrs Fraser ripped Moira's hand off her shoulder and raked her nails down the other woman's face, shouting, "Mistake? Mistake? Your fucking son is a mistake!"

With that she lunged towards Moira Harper and grabbed handfuls of her hair in her fists. Screaming wildly, she whipped Moira's head from side to side. The policeman stood there in shock for several seconds and then, gathering his wits, pulled Helen Fraser away and restrained her with a huge bear hug. Moira Harper sagged back against the patrol car, hair wild and blood streaking her face where the fingernails had torn her skin.

Not one of the other mothers came over to her or offered an explanation of what had happened. Indeed, they stood staring at her like she was a leper, surrounding their children in a protective huddle. Eventually Moira staggered back over to the policeman who was holding her son down. She pleaded with him to tell her what had happened but to no avail- the policeman merely told her she might want to contact a lawyer. Moira Harper fell to the ground again and started to sob.

Soon enough the other mothers had whisked their children away, the police and ambulance left and Moira was alone, crumpled on the driveway. She lay there until dusk fell and then somehow found the strength to stagger home where she again collapsed on the verandah. She lay there for uncountable minutes until Merv flicked on the light and shouted what did she think she was doing lying there like that and to get inside and get his tea. Despite knowing Merv could easily (and often did) use his hands to hurry her up, Moira found that she physically could not get up. She looked up at her husband of so many years and howled like a wolf. Merv, for once surprised out of his usual temper, bent down to her, scooped her up and deposited her on the couch.

In the days after Dunstan was taken away, Moira did little other than weep and wail. Merv continued to go to work as normal and beyond once muttering 'I told you that boy was no use', he remained silent over the whole incident. Moira was constantly down at the lockup where her baby boy was being held. The lawyer told her that the police didn't know what to do with him – he couldn't be charged with murder because he could not understand what he had done. They were considering sending him to a mental institution but this didn't seem right either.

Eventually, Dunstan was released without charge and went home with his mummy. Of course, after such an incident, the Harpers could not stay in the town where they had always lived. They were forced to move away and start fresh in a place where no-one knew what had happened. Moira was grateful for this new chance and again started watching her boy day and night for any sign of misbehaviour. None being forthcoming, she again began to let him out to play with the neighbourhood children. She felt sure that he had learned his lesson and that nothing bad would come of this.

Pink slip.

He was up, showered and dressed by 6am – same as every other day for the last 30 years. The only difference now was that there wasn't actually anywhere to go. The factory had slowly and consistently downsized over about three years until finally there was only a handful of staff left.

He could still remember every detail of the day the boss had given him the pink slip...thirty five years at the company – never once late and only two days off ever and that had been when his mother had passed on. But now, here was Stan (as familiar as his own face), telling him he had been laid off.

"Early retirement hey mate," he said, trying to make light of it, but knowing his own pink slip wasn't far off.

That night he had gone home clutching the last cheque he would receive from the job he had worked at since he was 16 years old.

"Should frame it," he'd said when he threw it on the table, "Or burn it."

Meryl had not been very sympathetic either – no dinner on the table and no shoulder to cry on. "Righto," she'd said, slapping on her hat, "I'm off to bingo."

And off she went, leaving him to wallow in his own misery in front of a plate of baked beans, his mood black and tears rolling unbidden down his cheeks. After his solitary dinner he had retired to his bed and been unable to get up for anything other than nature's calling and to eat every now and then.

It had gone on in this manner for a few weeks, until Meryl had finally snapped at him and told him in no uncertain terms to get up out of bed and get over it.

"You're only unemployed, you're not dead," she'd spat.

"May as well be," he'd replied sourly. A man without work is hardly a man at all.

Weeks had continued to go by, turning into months. He would get up; shower, dress in his work clothes and sit in the lounge room all day looking at the walls, watching the hands on the clock make their lazy circles. He would mark off smoko at 10am, lunch at 1pm and knock off at 5pm. He would then shower again, put his robe and slippers on and return to the chair in front of the fire.

Meryl would bustle in and out, day after day, dusting and cleaning around him like one more piece of furniture. Mostly she would ignore him but occasionally she would drop acid comments about the shameful thing he had become.

Finally one day in December, some time between smoko and lunch, she had bustled in with a suitcase in each hand. She had set them down at his feet and laid a cool hand on his face. "You need to go," she'd said, and for the first time in a long time, her voice had been gentle.

He remembered looking into her pale blue eyes, confusion and then understanding and sorrow filling him.

"Laid off by the job and the wife, all in one year," he'd say later, making a weak attempt to smile.

So he had gone, without argument. What could he have said to erase the disgust in her eyes? He ended up at the YMCA, which had rooms cheap for single men. Single. After 30 years of marriage, this was not a word that sat easily in his mouth. He was a man who took his vows seriously – hadn't he sworn in front of the church and half the town to provide for Meryl? He felt in his heart that if he couldn't uphold his promises, then it was right that he should go.

The days went on, stretching out in front of him, much the same as before, him being unable to break the habit of getting up early for a days work that would not eventuate. Long days were spent marking time with other men who had nothing to do and nowhere to go. He sometimes left the day room to walk the dawn lit streets and ponder his options. Although he had registered as unemployed and looked at the classifieds each day, getting another job was not a thought that he really entertained. How could a man with a ninth grade education and no real skills other than a strong back and a willingness to put in a days labour, hope to find something when blokes half his age weren't working?

It was not in his nature to go on the dole, and there was no way he could go home to Meryl without a pay cheque to give her each week. It seemed that in any real sense, his life was over at the age of 51.

It was only another day, same as all the others, when he drove his old Holden (same car for 23 years, lovingly polished and maintained), out to the bush and parked it in the shade of an old gum tree. No sense in letting the sun bake the paint, even now. "Old habits die hard," he thought with a small smile.

He sat down on a fallen log, and put the barrel into his mouth. It tasted oily and metallic, cool even in the heat of the day. He glanced at his watch – five minutes to five, he noted. He put the gun down and waited the last five minutes. He imagined he could hear the whistle blowing, tools being put down and men laughing. He nodded once, it was all as it should be. He then proceeded to issue himself the final pink slip of his life.

Heinsteele.

The day the welfare came knocking was the same as any other to Heinsteele – he had gotten up at 7am as usual, fed and clothed himself and the boy and set out the day's lessons. This routine was interrupted at about 9am by the persistent ringing of the doorbell. Heinsteele finally flung open the door.

-Yes?

A thin middle aged woman in a dowdy suit stood there. She was carrying a clipboard and briefcase and her mouth was pinched tight in annoyance.

-Oh well, you are home then I see. I am Elizabeth Ross from the welfare department. May I come in?

-What for?

-I have come to see about the child – your son is he?

-What about him?

The woman shifted awkwardly and consulted her clipboard.

-Perhaps we can discuss this inside Mr um…uh…Heinsteele?

Heinsteele stood aside and let the woman into the hallway, shutting the door behind her and leading her into the kitchen.

-Right. What is it about the boy then?

Elizabeth Ross sat at the table and opened her briefcase. She pulled out a file and a shiny pen.

-Well, I will need some details and then I will need to see the child.

Heinsteele abruptly left the room, returning with a boy, pale faced and slim. He was dressed neatly in a collared shirt and pants, brown hair a little long over wide eyes. Heinsteele indicated that the boy should sit down.

-Hello there. Whats your name then?

The boy did not answer.

-Oh, shy are you? Well I am Elizabeth and I am here to find out a bit about you. What is your name dear?

-The boy doesn't speak.

Her eyes snapped up.

-What do you mean he doesn't speak? Why doesn't he speak?

-He just doesn't.

-Oh a bit like *that* is he?

Her finger twirled against her temple.

-No he is not! He just doesn't speak. Hasn't done for a good 2 years.

-Well, I can't say I have ever heard of that before. How old is he?

-He looks to be about 9 wouldn't you say?

The woman again swung startled eyes around.

-What? Don't you know how old he is?

-I said he looks to be around 9.

-This is very peculiar indeed Mr Heinsteele. The boy may or may not be your son, he doesn't speak and you don't seem to know how old he is. Very odd. How do you explain this?

-I don't.

-What do you mean, you don't? I am asking you to explain.

-Look, what is this about? What is your business here?

The woman shuffled some papers and consulted her notes.

-We have reports that an elderly man and a school aged child have moved in. The child has not enrolled in nor attended any school in the area and no-one seems to know anything about either of them. People are understandably concerned. We need to establish who he is and where he belongs.

-He belongs here.

-Is he your son then?

-No.

-Well what relation is he to you? Where are his parents and how did he come to stay with you?

-The boy belongs here with me – his parents are gone.

-What do you mean gone? Are they dead? And so you would be the grandfather then?

-Ok.

-Well are you or aren't you, Mr Heinsteele?

-I said ok.

-Well, ok then, why doesn't he – what is his name anyway – you do know that I presume?

-Thomas

-Thomas what?

-Just Thomas.

-Why isn't he in school?

-He does his lessons here, with me.

-A teacher are you?

-No

-Well then…

She looked up expectantly but was met with silence and a stony face.

-Why doesn't he speak? Is he retarded? Deaf perhaps?

-He is not deaf and he is certainly not retarded. He just doesn't speak.

-Doesn't or can't?

-Whichever – does it matter?

-Of course it matters Mr Heinsteele – if he can, then he should.

-Why?

She looked up again, startled and indignant.

-Why? Why? Because that is how normal people communicate – normal people speak. How can you communicate if he doesn't speak? How do you know when he is ill or hungry or wants something?

-I know

-How do you know Mr Heinsteele?

-I just know

-Well then, do you not think he at least has the right to an education? To go to school and mix with other children? To learn?

-He learns

-What about learning to be among others – can you teach him that too, can you?

-He has learnt enough about others.

Elizabeth Ross threw down her pen in exasperation.

-Really Mr Heinsteele! You are being very un-cooperative. I do not want to have to take the boy into care to get some answers from you. Now please! Who is this boy and how did he come to be in your care?

-You want to know so much don't you? Well know this...

Heinsteele stood and went around the table. He gently urged the boy to stand and pushed his shirtsleeve up to reveal a skinny arm, mottled and scarred with purple half moons and old welts. He then turned the boy around, raising his shirt to display his back, a criss-cross map of yellowed bruises and scars.

The woman sucked in air in shock. Heinsteele looked into her eyes and leaned close.

-Know this. This is what he has learned from others.

-Who did this to him?

Heinsteele lowered the boy's shirt and led him from the room, ruffling his hair gently.

-Finish your lessons.

He returned to the table and sat down.

-Well Mr Heinsteele – who did this to him? How did he get these injuries?

-I believe the burns are from cigarettes and the scars from a length of hose. Some of them are from being tied up and some are from being thrashed. He is skinny because he doesn't eat much – he is used to going without and is frightened to take too much.

-Who did this? You?

-Hardly

-Who then?

-I believe that the boy's mother and her assortment of motley boyfriends liked to take their amusement from the boy's suffering

-Where are these people now?

-Look Ms Ross – the boy has had some terrible experiences and he is now in my care; that should be sufficient.

-Mr Heinsteele, it is most certainly not sufficient. What will I write on my report? I need to know where and who the boy's parents are and whether you have a legal right to care for the boy.

-I may not be the boy's blood and I may not have legal rights but he stays here. The parents are dead if you must know.

-Now see here – if the situation is as you say it is, the boy is an orphan and must be taken into state care.

-I can't allow that

-I am not asking you Mr Heinsteele – these are laws – it is my job to ensure that the boy is safe.

Heinsteele slammed his fist down on the table.

-Where were you when the boy was being burned and starved and whipped? Where were you when he spent days tied up and locked in a cupboard? Where were you when he cried for help and crawled through a broken window to reach my house?

The woman looked exasperated, her eyes rolling heavenwards.

-Mr Heinsteele, surely you understand, we have protocols and procedures – we cannot simply race around peering through windows and taking children from their parents on the off chance they are being abused.

His voice was low and dangerous.

-An off chance?

-Well you know, many people make false allegations and then homes are disrupted... and really Mr Heinsteele! With the parents is usually the best place for children. I have been a social worker for 20 years and I always like to give the benefit of the doubt – I find that the children can tend to exaggerate – one flick on the bottom and they call the welfare. Some of them need a smack now and then, wouldn't you agree Mr Heinsteele.

-How many smacks do you think a child would need to be scarred like the boy is? After looking at him, how can you believe that anything he might say would be exaggerated?

-Well clearly, yes, there has been some harsh treatment in this case. We are not condoning that of course. Now we will be aiming to rectify the situation by taking him to a safe place and seeing about finding him a new family.

-He is in a safe place and I am his family now.

-Well Mr Heinsteele, you could certainly make an application to the court to seek custody. I'm not sure how successful you would be given that you are a single man...and well over the age we would normally recommend...but you would certainly be welcome to try your luck.

Briskly she began to tidy her things.

-Would you please get a bag ready for Thomas so I can take him with me now? He will be in a nice home by the weekend.

-I'm afraid I can't let you do that Ms Ross. I would thank you to leave my property now.

- Mr Heinsteele really! We don't want this to have to get ugly now do we?

She smiled with what she must have thought was a winning smile.

-Lets not be silly – we all know what is best for little Thomas don't we?

-I'm not going!

Both Heinsteele and Elizabeth Ross swung around in shock at the rusty but forceful sound of the child's voice. He stood, fists clenched, behind the chair in which the social worker sat.

- Now Thomas, I know you have been happy here with Mr Heinsteele, but now you are going to come along with me and I will find you a lovely family to stay with. You may even have brothers and sisters or a little dog. What do you think?

The boy moved with lightening speed and before either of the adults could move, he had a kitchen knife clutched in his little hand.

-I won't go. I won't.

Before they could move he had lurched forward and thrust the knife deep into the back of the social worker. Her eyes bulged in shock as she fell forward on the table – blood spewing from her and splashing over her clipboard and notes. He then flung himself around Heinsteele's legs and clung to him.

-I won't leave you. I won't go to another family.

Heinsteele sighed heavily. He looked at the rapidly expiring form of Elizabeth Ross and with resignation, his mind started to work. He started to think how they could cover this one up, where they could go next.

-Its ok Thomas, you won't be going anywhere without me. Go and get your things together – we must leave tonight.

Heart heavy, Heinsteele began to pack his belongings. 10 moves in 2 years. 2 drunken parents left for dead in a burning house and 2 dead social workers since – where would it ever end? The boy clearly had problems but obviously Heinsteele couldn't leave him now even if he wanted to.

The second youngest son.

The day seemed too warm and beautiful for the occasion. Fluffy white clouds drifted in an aqua blue sky, while the barest of breezes ruffled the leaves on the fine old eucalypts that stood guard at the gates.

People milled about; more people than one might have expected. Stiff and uncertain. Dressed in their black best. Even the children were unnaturally still and quiet, formal in small suits and shiny shoes.

Family stood in one clump, nearest the gates and the others clotted into groups who made stilted conversations about subjects of little consequence. Whispers about the weather and other matters started and then died out, leaving the speakers shuffling and uncomfortable.

The long black car slid up, silent. Silencing the crowd. The doors opened and forced out the widowed man and his four sons, who stood dazed and blinking in the bright gaze of the sun. The back doors of the hearse opened and revealed the simple black coffin, silver handles shiny; like water in the light.

Somehow, without words or direction, the gathering assembled and followed the family who carried their wife and mother through the headstones to an open grave surrounded by freshly turned earth.

The man and his sons placed the coffin down with infinite gentleness and stood solemn and still. The second youngest boy must have been feeling not only grief, but guilt, because it had been he who was driving the car that his mother was killed in.

The rest of the mourners huddled around the grave and let the drone of the minister wash over them as he sketched the life of the woman who lay before them. It wasn't a long life, but the achievements were many and in her passing, it was revealed a portrait of a woman needed by many and cherished by all.

As the words drew to a close and the coffin was lowered, the husband threw himself forward; blind in his grief, attempting to rejoin his beloved.

The two eldest sons held him as he wept, and on the verge of collapse in his agony, he brought tears to the eyes of everyone present.

The second youngest boy stood nearby, dry-eyed in his sorrow. He scooped up a handful of earth and trickled it down onto the coffin. His back was straight and stiff as his brothers and father clung together. Not one of the others opened their arms to him and so he stood alone at the head of the grave. He was not intentionally excluded but nor was he given the same warmth – because everyone knew why they were burying his mother. No-one, least of all himself, would ever forget or be able to separate him from the tragedy of her death. Some of those there and most of all himself, wished it had been him instead. Or at least him as well. As penance. Instead of this guilt that he would carry for his whole life.

The coffin was lowered to its final resting place and all of the prayers were said. Some of the mourners began to trickle away, while those closest to the grave were unwilling or unable to turn away in the face of so much pain and stayed, offering useless words of sorrow to the family.

Finally when all the tears were dry and all the comfort given, people hurried out of the cemetery, loosening ties and plucking at itchy dresses. Talk turned to ordinary things and a woman who meant so much a few minutes ago was pushed to the back of minds filled with the more pressing issues of the living.

The man.

Clem Edwards was THE MAN. He had long known that there was something special about himself, that he was somehow *more* than everyone else. He knew he was THE MAN because he could do whatever he wanted, whenever he wanted, and no-one could do anything about it. He even had a sign in his house that said 'If you don't like it; get the fuck out!' This was Clem Edwards' personal motto and he prided himself on not taking shit from anyone.

People who tried to give him shit or tried to stop him from doing what he wanted to do got *FIXED*. THE MAN had many ways that he could *FIX* people – for example, if his wife spoke out of turn he would beat the crap out of her. For her own good of course, so she could learn. Of course, he wasn't always this understanding – he often slit throats, gouged out eyes, removed limbs and generally messed up anyone who crossed him.

Clem Edwards had not always been THE MAN – before he was THE MAN, he was only a small weak little boy who had spent long days locked in an airless closet with no food or drink. Little Clem knew very well that he was the bane of his fathers existence and often suffered whippings and beatings that would last for hours. Clem's father had a talent for language and would curse his son with every name under the sun, telling him night and day that he was worthless and that he hated him. Clem's father seemed to delight in depriving and torturing him – 'you gotta learn to be a man' he would scream as he held him down and burned him with cigars or held his head under water in the sink or swung that electrical cord against his bare back again and again. Once Clem had watched his father set his beloved cat on fire and then chase it around with a shovel, finally smashing its skull against the ground. Clem vowed then and there, that when he was grown up, he would never be at anyone's mercy again.

Once little Clem got big enough; the next time his father got the whip out, Clem turned and wrenched it from his father's hand , enjoying the look of surprise and terror on his face. It was at that point that Clem realised that he never had to be afraid again – as long as he could make other people afraid of him.

Since that day, Clem took it upon himself to make sure that everyone was afraid of him. And when Clem Edwards was fully grown and had finally become a man, he took it upon himself to become THE MAN and to turn his talent for *FIXING* people into a career. THE MAN was somewhat of a hired gun - although unpredictable and uncontrollable – he would *FIX* people for a price (and if he felt like it). Sometimes THE MAN would FIX people just because he wanted to.

On this particular day, THE MAN was driving home from a job interstate when he saw a fancy Mercedes convertible about 50 metres ahead, double parked right in his lane, at peak hour no less – cars banked alongside him and no chance of changing lanes.

"Son-of-a-bitch!" he screamed, spit flying from his mouth in a long arc. "Cant you see this is a motherfucking clear way?"

THE MAN accelerated, slamming his Humvee into the rear of the parked car, forcing it up onto the sidewalk and crushing it against a dumpster. He then reversed and rammed it again and again until the car was beyond repair. Luckily his vehicle was fitted with a heavy duty bull bar just for these kinds of situations and the Hummer remained unmarked. Satisfied that the car had been well and truly *FIXED*, THE MAN prepared to drive on.

Suddenly an obese, dishevelled woman ran out of a nearby store, shrieking, wailing and gesticulating in his direction; her flabby arms whipping and waving with her every move. THE MAN looked up, surprised and incredulous – surely this disgusting creature was not addressing him? But yes! The stupid woman had the gall to come right up to his window and bellow in at him – her fetid breath washing over him in acrid waves.

"You'll pay for this you bastard – I'll sue your ass!"

THE MAN smiled. "Is that right?" he asked softly, opening the door and stepping out. He was immaculately dressed and groomed as always, and the sight of this grossly overweight thing in her curlers and housedress so repulsed him that that he almost didn't want to touch her.

Almost.

THE MAN smiled again, soothingly. He spoke politely, "You want this *FIXED?* Is that what you are saying madam?"

The woman screamed right into his face, spraying flecks of saliva and gesturing wildly, "Yes I want it fixed, I want it fixed right now you asshole!"

THE MAN reached into his pocket and pulled out a shiny straight edge razor. He flicked out his wrist and sliced the woman's face open from eyebrow to chin, a huge pulsing gash. He then twisted his hand slightly, opening up her nose in a long bloody slit. The woman had now, thankfully, stopped screaming obscenities and was trying to beat him off with ineffectual blows. With a graceful sweeping gesture, THE MAN glided the razor across her eyes, puncturing one and slicing the other neatly in two.

"Oh yes," he whispered into her ear "I will *FIX* it right now."

He pushed the huge, blind, bleeding mass to the ground and stepped over her, grimacing with distaste at the flecks of gore on his designer shirt. He slid back behind the wheel of the HumVee and carefully reversed. Engine screaming and tyres smoking, he raced up onto the kerb, slamming the woman into the tangled wreck of her car. He continued to do this three or four times, until she finally stopped moaning and grunting and had slumped over, a silent bloody mess.

As he pulled away, he gave a jaunty wave to the horrified onlookers and chuckled with satisfaction. He smoothed a hand over his still immaculate hair and winked at his reflection in the mirror, "I think its *FIXED* now Bitch", he hissed.

Roadkill

The trees hurtled by, all blurring into one fuzzy image as Brad Evans glanced sleepily over at his family – his wife Susan dozing against the window and twin girls asleep in the back. It had been a great holiday but it was a long trip home, through vast stretches of dark highway – he had already been driving for 5 hours straight and wanted to make it home that night if possible – only another 4 or 5 hours to go.

Brad felt his head growing heavy, eyelids like lead as he struggled to stay awake. The landcruiser bumped onto the shoulder of the road, sliding a little in the gravel, causing Susan to open one sleep filled eye. She elbowed Brad, breaking his slumber. He swung the cruiser back onto the road, shaking his head, trying to clear his thoughts. If only he wasn't so damn exhausted. He cranked the window and tried to let the chill night air wake him up.

He had only just shut his eyes for a second when the bright glare of a huge pair of headlights slammed him awake, the sound of an air horn sending shivers down his spine as an oil tanker barrelled past inches from the side of the landcruiser.

Brad panicked and overcompensated, sharply swinging the steering wheel, causing the gravely shoulder to rear up again. The tyres could find no grip in the slippery pebbles and the cruiser jolted and skidded as Brad struggled to bring it back onto the road. As he stared out of the windscreen, desperately trying to control the vehicle, the headlights seemed to pick up the glow of a pair of eyes. Before Brad could wonder at this, there was a dull thump on the hood, a louder thud on the roof, followed by a faint slap on the road.

Susan woke up fully then, eyes dull and staring and she craned around to peer out of the rear window.

"Brad? What..? Did we hit something? Honey..?"

Brad finally brought the landcruiser to a skidding standstill, some 50 metres from where the collision had occurred and turned, heart racing to look out at the blackness behind them. His breath came in short gasps and his forehead was beaded with sweat.

"I can't see anything. It must have been a kangaroo"

Susan looked over at him. "Well you better drag it off – we can't just leave it in the road."

Brad nodded, running a shaky hand over his hair and glancing into the back seat. Both children were sound asleep, undisturbed by the whole incident.

"Stay here" he said, grabbing the torch and opening the door.

He landed on the gravel with a crunch and headed for the front of the vehicle to check for damage first. The bull-bar had protected the lights and grill but there was a roundish dent in the hood and another on the roof. Just as Brad was turning to go see what he had hit, his eye was caught by a splash of colour. His blood ran cold as he realised it was a scrap of cloth hooked on the grill and spattered with blood. He looked up and met his wife's eyes through the windscreen – he could see her mouth moving, asking if everything was ok. He furtively plucked up the scrap of material, nodded brusquely and strode to the rear of the vehicle. He could see nothing but the inky blackness, broken only by the small circle of light the torch threw out. This strip of road was remote and unlit. A shiver ran down Brad's spine as he stepped forward along the road. He walked for what seemed like forever – he could see nothing, the road appeared to be clear.

Just as he was ready to turn back, a final sweep of the torch lit on a vague shape, humped in darkness on the shoulder of the road. Brad jogged up to it and nudged it with his foot, flipping it over and exposing it to the light. A pair of pale blue eyes stared up at him. Brad strangled a scream as he swept the light over the shape, revealing a deeply lined and tanned face and the lean body of a man who surely hadn't had a decent meal anytime lately. A backpack still clung to the man's back, spilling its contents into the pool of blood surrounding him.

Brad's initial horror soon turned to distaste as he gazed at the body - a hitchhiker, Brad supposed, a road rat, a bum, a loser. Trying for a ride on this dark and lonely stretch of road. Probably a man without family, friends or roots. A man who's death would most likely matter to no-one but which would cause all kinds of problems for Brad. His mind began to race, thinking about the consequences of what had happened – he might go to jail! Or at the very least, people would find out and turn it into some kind of scandal. Brad felt a flash of anger at the man – how dare he cause this situation?

As he stood there, mind whirling, the dim glow of the torch picked up a slight movement. The crumpled man's mouth was moving – he was trying to speak through a mouthful of dirt. Brad leant down and touched the man's neck – there was a faint pulse – thin and reedy but definitely there! The hitchhiker seemed to be having trouble breathing and a little blood seeped from the corner of his mouth. Punctured lung probably, Brad thought to himself. The man would most likely die, even with medical attention; and then the questions and accusations would start.

Brad considered the options – he could call for his wife to help load the man into the cruiser and rush him to the nearest hospital. He could grab his mobile phone and call for assistance. He could wait here with the man while his wife drove for help.

Then a black thought entered his mind – he could drag the hitchhiker off the road into the bushes and leave him there. Surely it wouldn't take long for the man to bleed out - what was the point of Brad rushing around if the man was going to die anyway? Who would know? Would it be worth going through all of the hassle and trauma, answering questions and maybe facing punishment, all for nothing? No-one had seen the accident and no-one could possibly link Brad to it when and if the bum was eventually found. Why should Brad and his family have to suffer because of one man's carelessness? Brad's thoughts spun rapidly out of control and he forced himself to calm down, to think logically.

It didn't take long to convince himself that this one transient man was not as important as Brad and his family. Brad decided it would not make sense to ruin their holiday and possibly their whole lives for the sake of this no-hoper. And after all, it's not like he was *killing* the man – he was going to die anyway – Brad was just letting nature take its course.

Satisfied with this final justification, Brad grabbed the man's feet and dragged him through the gravel and slung him behind a clump of bush growing off from the side of the road. He hurriedly scooped up the spilt items from the backpack, noting that there was what looked like an army medal and a creased photo of a little girl among the junk. He wondered at this briefly but then stuffed the things back into the backpack. Irritated, he brushed off the man's fingers as they clutched at him, ignoring his pleading eyes and garbled words.

Brad dusted his hands off and strode back to the cruiser, smiling at his wife.

"Yeah, we splatted a Kangaroo – nothing to worry about love"

Susan sighed with relief, "Oh thank God! You know, its silly but for a minute there I was scared we had hit a person! I mean, I don't know what someone would be doing out here at this time of night, but for a second I just thought...."

Brad chuckled and patted her arm. "Susan really! If someone actually had been out here and god forbid we had hit them, do you think I would just leave them here and drive away?"

They both laughed at the absurdity of that idea.

Brad snapped his seatbelt on, put the landcruiser into gear and pulled carefully back onto the road. He did not once look into the rear-view mirror and only the slightest trembling in his fingers reminded him what he had done.

Kev and Dave and me.

I've been called a lot of things in my life: loser, street-kid, bogan and bum are just a few. I would just call myself a loner if I had to choose one word to describe what I am. There are plenty of people who think they are my friends but I really only have only ever had two I would call true friends. I grew up with Dave and Kev and they were like brothers to me. I don't have any brothers or sisters of my own and my dad is dead. He was a cool old guy and when he died about 4 years ago, my mum just lost it. She's been in an out of the loony bin since then so I just stayed where I could – at Kev's mostly and bunking on other peoples couches other times. Some nights I spend in the park.

I never got to finish school and I know I'm not 'book smart' but I like to think I can hold my own on the street. I pick up a days work where I can but most people don't like the look of me. I usually have to do the shit jobs like digging ditches and hauling bricks. I'm not scared of hard work but I always dream of a fancy office job where I wouldn't sweat all day and fall in to bed dog tired every night. It would be nice to have a regular paycheck every week too and then I wouldn't have to go through the humiliation of standing in the dole line and taking handouts just to get by.

Maybe one day I'll get back to school – if I don't end up in jail or dead. Where I live you got more chance of ending up in one of those places than in Uni. My two mates never finished school either – around here you pretty much go through to year 10 and then you leave. They didn't have regular jobs either – they have the same problem I do – not many people want to look beneath the tough veneer to see whats underneath.

Kevin had the stereotypical bogan look; long black mullet hair and sly blue eyes. Black jeans, boots and flannel shirts were his daily uniform. He was kind of short but tough and muscly too. His hard looks are deceiving because he is truly a good person – a loyal friend with a soft heart. He would be a hell of a fighter – if only he would – he thinks things can mostly be solved without fists and knives and guns. He has a unique way of talking, he doesn't really say much but when he does he doesn't bullshit or beat around the bush. You can always rely on Kev for the truth. He also writes stories and poetry and when he's in the mood, or after a beer or two, he might read you some.

Kev's mum works long shifts at night and sleeps all day - his dad isn't around much, in and out of jail and running between two families. Kev complains about it sometimes but I just tell him he is lucky to have a mother around at all. He says that she never wanted him and that she blames him for ruining her life. I guess she did what a lot of girls do around here – have a baby young and get stuck here forever. I actually don't mind her though. She's always been good to me, never complains about me staying there and at least she's still sane which is more than I can say for my own mother.

On the other hand, Dave is kind of hard to describe – he plays so many different people. Some days he is serious and quiet and other days he keeps us in stitches with his jokes and the crazy things he does. I think he hides behind his personalities – he lies sometimes and he brags about how many people he has shot with this gun he stole from his old man. We all know he hasn't really shot anyone but we let it go because he is kind of insecure and needs to impress people. His home life hasn't been all that great either – his dad was a drunk and used to beat up him and his mum all the time. Plus his big brother got killed in a bike accident a few years back. I once heard his old man scream he'd wished it was Dave that had died rather than his brother. I know this cut Dave up real bad and only made him hate his father more. Ever since his mother died and his dad went to jail, he's been staying with some aunt over on the East side – all I know about her is that she's old, fat and permanently stoned. She lies on the couch all day swigging from a brown bag.

I still remember clearly the night when Dave's mum died. I was sleeping rough in the park, it was getting late and pretty cold so I was huddled down in the jacket my dad gave me before he died. Its pretty much the only part of my dad I had left and I planned to keep it forever. A running figure broke me out of thought and I grabbed my knife instinctively. Then I realised it was Dave. He ran right up to the wall where I was curled up. He was crying as he slammed his fists into the wall again and again. He finally stopped when his knuckles were battered and bleeding. He slid down the wall and just sat there sobbing. I was really confused – I had never seen Dave lose it like this before. He finally took a deep breath and started to talk. He told me that when he had gotten home that night, his mum was sitting at the table with another black eye and her face all bloody. This wasn't unusual in itself – it was Friday night which meant his dad would be drinking up his dole money and would be in a fighting mood. The only thing that was out of the ordinary was that she was holding a gun. Dave recognised the gun as one his dad kept in his bedside table and had thought that finally she had had enough and killed the old bastard. Dave says that in those few seconds, as he stood there thinking this, she put the gun to her own head and shot herself. He says that when the shot rang out, his old man staggered into the kitchen and when he saw what had happened he laughed! He actually laughed! Dave says he just grabbed the gun from his mothers hand and ran to the park, leaving his father in a drunken stupor laughing over his dead wife's body.

Later on that night, we heard the sirens as the ambulance and police went past and Dave just kept crying and crying. At one point he held the gun cocked to his own head and spoke in a low serious voice about ending it all. I didn't know what to say or do so I just held him in my arms as he sobbed. Eventually he threw that gun far across the grass and just lay there silent. We must have fallen asleep at some point but when I woke up the next day, Dave was gone and stayed gone for over two weeks.

We didn't ask him where he'd been or what he'd done but things were different with Dave since that night – he was a little more crazy and he carried that gun every where with him. He swore he'd use it if he needed to and we began to believe him. He started to pick fights and drink a lot every day, starting in the morning just like his old man. Dave really isn't a happy drunk – he gets louder and meaner as he drinks and I think he actually gets a little insane. Sometimes I think he's turning in to his old man, although I'd never say that to him.

One night we were sitting around outside the local shop, passing a bottle and talking crap. This was normal – like everyone in our town, we had nothing to do and nowhere to go so we planned to just get drunk and hang out. Kev and I were a little tipsy but Dave must have been really slugging it back because he was wrecked. He started swearing and singing filthy songs at the top of his voice. Kev and I thought this was hilarious and rolled around on the ground laughing until the shop owner came out and then things got ugly real fast. He told us to clean up our language or leave. Dave faced up to him and told him that we weren't going anywhere. The shopkeeper began to mutter something about teaching us a lesson and started to roll up his sleeves. The shopkeeper was an old guy in his 50's but hard and muscled like he still lifted weights or something. He had jailhouse tattoos on his forearms and an evil glint in his eyes. This didn't stop Dave who got right up close and laughed in the guys face.

The shopkeeper warned us that we had one more chance to leave but Dave just kept laughing. The shopkeeper raised his fists and moved forward with a smirk on his face and murder in his eyes. Suddenly his face paled to a milky colour and his eyes bulged. It was then that I saw that Dave had that gun pressed into the guy's ribs. Kev and I jumped and up and started shouting at him to stop but Dave just kept on laughing. He raised the gun to the guys head and pulled the trigger again and again. The sound of the empty clicking noise must have brought the shopkeeper back to reality because he grabbed Dave by the throat, lifted him off the ground and threw him against the window. Dave managed to gasp out some words that stopped the man cold - he told him that the next bullet was live. The shopkeeper released his grip on Dave's throat and he fell back against the shop wall, gasping for air.

Kev the peace-maker then pushed himself in between the shopkeeper and Dave and demanded that Dave give him the gun. When he got no response, he grabbed it from Dave's hands. He told the shopkeeper to get inside and stay there which he did, but minutes later we heard police sirens and ran like hell.

We raced to the park and lay there in silence, gasping for breath and staring at the sky. I suddenly felt stone cold sober and full of disbelief at what had happened. When I asked Dave why he had done that, he just laughed and said 'Why not?' My head was spinning and it wasn't the alcohol. Dave was showing a new, scary side of himself that I wasn't sure I liked. He just kept on laughing and asking us if we had ever seen anything like that before. I had to admit that I hadn't and secretly I knew I sure as hell never wanted to see it again either. Kev tried to talk some sense into Dave but Dave wasn't listening and eventually even he gave up.

Some time passed after that and Dave didn't pull the gun again but I could tell that something wasn't right inside him and I could feel the pressure building. For once, I felt I couldn't really talk to Kev about what was going on – he had got himself a girlfriend and had started to hang out with another crowd so we weren't seeing him that often. Kev had always been the one I could talk to – his rough looks belied a sensitive nature and he had a good ear for listening. Dave wasn't much for talking – he was fun to hang out with but wasn't much for the 'deep and meaningfuls'.

So nothing got said and Dave and I just continued to hang out as usual. One night we had gone down to the beach to watch the cars do burn outs and run drag races. We kind of 'borrowed' a car off the street to get there. Neither of us had a license but neither of us much cared. We were just sitting there in the car, smoking and watching the action when someone tapped on the window. I rolled it down about 10cm to see what they wanted. It was this guy Wayne from around our neighbourhood – he ran with a gang and was considered to be a pretty tough guy. By the look on his face and the words he used, he was pretty unhappy with us. He told us that the car we were sitting in belonged to one of his mates. He reached through the gap in the window, opened the door and pulled me out.

Wayne slammed me up against the side of the car and told me in no uncertain terms that I had better get away from the car. Dave slipped around to stand next to us – for once he didn't seem to be in a fighting mood and started to crack jokes to try to lighten the situation. Wayne wasn't amused and kept a hold of me and continued to spit abuse into my face. Then Wayne's buddy Butch loomed up beside us and started to get in on the action, swearing and threatening to kick our asses. Dave started to get riled up then and it looked like he was ready for a fight. Butch shoved him in the chest and made some crack about Dave's mother being a whore. I knew instantly then that this was going to end badly – I was only glad that he had left his gun at home. Dave told Butch that he had two seconds to take back what he said. Butch just laughed and repeated the remarks. It was then that Dave suddenly slammed his fist into Butch's face three times in quick succession. His nose spurted blood and his front tooth cracked but still Dave kept punching and punching - the whole time he was screaming at Butch to apologise.

Wayne and I just stood there frozen in shock until finally Butch fell to the ground. Dave kicked him in the stomach and slowly ground his foot on Butch's right hand, breaking his fingers with a sickening crunch. He then spat in his face and turned to look at Wayne – Dave asked if *he* had anything he wanted to say. Because Wayne isn't the smartest guy around and I guess because those gang guys have to stick together; he made some crack about Butch being right about Dave's mum. Dave just smiled a tight bleak grin and smashed Wayne in the face with a right hook that knocked him flat down on the ground. Because neither one of them looked like they were getting up, we tossed the keys to the car on the ground in front of them and headed home on foot.

Walking home, Dave asked me if what he had done was wrong. I told him I would have done the same thing. And even thought I don't know my mother anymore, I would have. It may have been true that his mother made some money on her back, but still...your mother is your mother. Whether she is a whore or she is crazy or just dead.

Well...word got around pretty fast, but what you hear isn't always the truth. I heard several rumours; some said Dave and I ran over Butch in the car; others said that Dave had beaten Butch up with a tyre iron; some said I had started the whole thing. The only rumour I heard that I knew was true was that Butch and Wayne and their crowd were out for our blood. I knew this was true because I ran into Butch one day at the shops; complete with a new bump in his nose, cast on his hand and an ugly look in his eyes. He didn't touch me right then but he made it clear that it was only a matter of time.

A few days later, we told Kev what had happened and of course he said he would stick by us. He too had been threatened by Butch and had wondered why. We kind of tried to get ourselves prepared for anything that might go down. Dave had that gun and I had the old switchblade. Kev refused to carry a weapon – he always said a fair fight isn't about knives and guns and someone dying. I wasn't sure how he could say that because in our neighbourhood there were no rules for fighting and no-one played fair.

A few long hot months went by and although nothing happened, everyone seemed tense and we were always on edge, waiting. It was late in the summer by then and the days were endless and stifling. Dave's old man was out of jail again and Dave was back living with him. Dave and I were hanging out in the park again one day trying to stay out of his way, when the little blonde chick Kev had been seeing came running up to us. She was crying and almost hysterical, telling us that she and Kev had been hanging at the Rec Centre when three guys had started hassling him. She said that they had taken a few punches at him but that he wouldn't fight back and so she had come to find us.

We ran to the Rec where we found Kev sprawled on the ground, surrounded by Butch, Wayne and another guy. They were laughing and swearing, calling for Kev to get up and fight. It was then I saw the blood on Kev's face – he had been cut open from eyebrow to jaw and had the startings of a black eye. We stepped up to them and told them to back off. We saw that Butch had the knife and the others had knuckle dusters on. I put my hand into my pocket to make sure my blade was there and I knew Dave had the gun with him and could maybe use it scare them off. We were just about to get into it when Kev stood up. He held his hands out palms up, staggering a little, and said that he didn't want to fight. The others just looked at each other and laughed. Then Butch sprang forward and slammed his fist into Kev's face, knocking him to the ground again.

I grabbed Butch and slammed him back into the wall. He kept laughing and flicked out his knife which he held under my chin. He slid it back and forth softly, just breaking the skin and causing a trickle of blood to run down my neck. He asked me if I was ready to die. I just stood there, bleeding and breathing for a minute and then raised my knee hard into his groin. He went down and I grabbed his blade and hurled it away, kicking him in the ribs for good measure. I heard a sickening crunch and knew that his ribs were broken. I brought my boot back again and slammed it into his stomach. I then turned to the others, ready to keep fighting, but no-one stepped forward.

Dave just looked at me and smiled – I saw that he had his gun out and pointed at Wayne. Wayne was pale and gasping for air as Dave cocked the pistol. I know for sure that he would have killed Wayne right then if Kev hadn't leapt up off the ground and at the gun. He knocked it off aim and sent the bullet ricocheting into the wall. Wayne and the other guy took this opportunity to grab Butch and run.

Kev started screaming at Dave about pulling the gun again and Dave faced up to him. I was sure at any minute that my two best friends were going to rip each others throats out. I tried unsuccessfully to get between them and everything was just wild, screaming chaos until suddenly Kev backed off and held his hand out to Dave. Dave stared at it for a long time before he took it. They shook and everything seemed ok again for the moment. Kev started talking about fighting not solving anything and how he had been trying to patch things up with Butch and his crew. Dave and I could not understand why he would want to do this – we eventually went to Kev' house where he kept talking long into the night but we never saw eye to eye on that.

Early the next morning as we sat on Kev's verandah and watched the sun come up, he told us that his girlfriend Randi was pregnant. We were about as shocked as you can get – not that we thought Kev was an angel or anything but we never expected him to knock some chick up at the age of 18. Neither Dave nor I knew the girl very well – she looked a little cheap and hard to me. She had a bit of a rep around town – some called her the town bike. She always looked pretty stoned and although neither of us wanted to ask Kev if he was sure the baby was his we were both thinking it. Kev seemed pretty happy though – he kept smiling and acting like this was the best thing that could happen to him. He gave us a big spiel about this baby giving his life some meaning and direction. Dave and I were pretty bewildered about the whole situation but didn't let on. After we left, we talked about it and agreed that it was just downright weird.

Later that week I dropped over to see Kev and to try and suss the situation out a bit more. His chick opened the door and told me he wasn't home but that I could come in and wait. Her eyes were huge and glassy and the house reeked of pot. The first thing she did was open a beer and offer me a bong. I declined and sat down on the couch. She sat down right next to me and smiled up at me. I was pretty uncomfortable and after about 10 minutes of stilted conversation and having to constantly move her hand off my leg, I finally asked her what we had all been wondering. I blurted, "This baby isn't Kev's is it?' She looked at me, startled and answered a shade too fast, "Yeah, course it is. Who else's would it be?"

Anyones! I thought. But I kept silent and just looked at her.

After that, she moved to another chair and chewed her nails. I fiddled with a magazine and we both just sat there in silence until Kev finally came home.

When he came in, I sprang up, relieved to be out of this awkward situation and Randi flounced off, clearly miffed at me. I took the opportunity to talk to Kev in private, trying to get a feel for what was happening. I tried to play it cool but lost it after not very long – demanding to know what was going on. I asked Kev straight out whether this baby was his and after some hesitation, he admitted that she was already pregnant when they met. He said that she was so sweet and helpless that he couldn't leave her, even though he felt nervous about becoming a father, especially to a baby that wasn't technically his. I had a very bad feeling about the whole thing and told him so. I felt that our years of friendship could withstand the honesty and that I owed him that. I told him about her rep around town and asked him if he was into any of the drugs that I had heard she was into. He just laughed and said that he didn't do that shit. He tried to calm me down and said that Randi was just into pot and that it was nothing to worry about.

So I left, and although I should have felt better hearing it from his own mouth, I couldn't escape the feeling that he was lying just as fast as he could. A few days later, I decided to do a bit of detective work and took a walk down to the rec centre. The lawn in front of the rec was littered with rubbish and in between all the junk lay a couple of guys, skinny, dirty and clearly wasted. I walked up to one of them and nudged him with my shoe, "Hey man, do you know Kevin Harris?"

The guy finally sat up, peering at me with red rimmed eyes, "He aint here" he slurred, "But I can fix you up until he gets here if you want"

Alarm bells rang in my mind, "What have you got?" I asked, trying to suss out the situation.

He dug into his pocket and pulled out, among other things, a syringe that looked well used. "I've got Go'ey or Horse – depends if you wanna go fast or slow!" he cackled.

"Does Kev sell you this?" I demanded.

His bloodshot eyes opened a fraction wider and he looked at me suspiciously, "Are you a cop?" he spluttered.

I laughed, looking down at my black jeans and flannel shirt, "Do I look like a cop?"

He smiled a big spaced out smile, "Nah man, you aint a cop – I can tell! But this is all I got right now – Kev can get you whatever you want though – trips, E, pot, whatever!"

I smiled a wry smile and said, "Is that right? Well I guess I'll just wait till I catch up with him then" I started to walk away and then turned back, "By the way – do you know a chick called Randi?"

He chuckled and said, "Oh yeah man, I know that bitch. She sells it too but not dope, if you know what I mean!"

I knew exactly what he meant. I said goodbye to the guy and headed back to the park so I could think. I couldn't believe this! Kev was dealing drugs and his girlfriend was a whore. No wonder he got so sensitive about it.

To tell the truth, I didn't care that much about Kev selling drugs – in our neighbourhood; you did what you had to do to get by. The only concern I had was whether he was using them too. And Randi! She probably didn't even know who the father was.

That night, I definitely didn't want to sleep at Kev's. I didn't think I could look him in the eye and I know I couldn't have looked at Randi, let alone acted as though everything was normal. So, I walked over to Dave's to see if I could stay there. I could hear his old man ranting and raving from the street but thought 'what the hell' and knocked anyway. Dave opened the door and he looked pretty happy to see me.

Pretty soon, it was clear why – his old man was drunk and in fine form. I came in and nodded to him. He just snorted in my direction and muttered something about the no-good losers that Dave hung out with. He then belched and yelled, "When are you gonna get a job and be a real man mate? Get some real friends instead of losers like Dave here?" He started to laugh loudly and continued to gulp his beer and burp intermittedly. A real class act. I thought then, and I still think now; If being a 'real man' means getting to be fat and forty and having nothing to do but drink beer and be an asshole, I would rather be a no-good loser forever!

After another screaming fight with his old man, we left and decided to sleep in the park again. We settled in and I told Dave about Kev and Randi and the whole drug thing. Dave said nothing we could say would stop him selling and all we could do was hope he wasn't using it too. I knew he was right because even though I thought about it all night I figured the only thing we could do to stop him was to turn him in to the cops. I just couldn't do that. Also part of me knew that he had to make money somehow and in this neighbourhood, you do what you have to. Over the next few weeks I asked Kev again and again if he was using but each time he swore he wasn't.

The next few months seemed to pass quickly and we didn't see that much of Kev, only in passing and always with Randi. She got bigger and bigger but clearly was still taking whatever drugs she was taking and Kev kept insisting he was sticking by her.

I was hanging out down at the rec one Saturday when I saw a friend of Randi's who told me that Randi had gone into labour that morning. The girl was pretty wasted but I gathered from her that Randi had refused to go to the hospital and was insistent on having the baby at home even though it must have been weeks and weeks premature.

I ran to Kev's as fast as I could, frantically trying to call Dave on my mobile on the way. I only got his message bank and so I turned up there alone. One of Randi's dopey friends was guarding the door and wouldn't let me past even though I threatened to smash his face in. He was too stoned to care I think.

So I sat there on the front steps for what seemed like hours until finally Kev came out. I was stunned to see that he wasn't smiling – he was crying. "Kev!" I shouted, "I've been here for fucking hours mate! Is it born? Is it a boy or a girl?"

He just looked at me and I have never seen eyes as dead as his. "It was a boy" he said.

I just stared at him in utter confusion. *Was* a boy? His shoulders shook and he turned away from me, sobbing and clutching the railing of the verandah. He spoke in a weird, halting staccato "He died mate. I saw him born and it was so beautiful. It was a miracle. I held him. He didn't breathe. I watched him die. I couldn't do anything. A boy mate, a boy."

He started crying hard then and I put my arms around him. We sat on his front steps and he stared into nothing for what seemed like hours, eventually speaking;

"He wasn't mine, I know that. I didn't care because I wanted him anyway. I would have loved him like my own – I would have done anything for him."

I knew it wasn't the time to ask but I couldn't help myself, "Is that why you were dealing?"

He looked at me with eyes that were weary but not surprised, "Yeah mate. I had nothing and when I sell the shit, I can make a lot. I was saving it all so he could have everything he needed." He started to cry again then, "But fuck! I couldn't even give him his life – what the fuck was I gonna give him with a few bucks?"

I tried to console him by telling him it wasn't his fault – I told him that if the nurse couldn't save him, Kev certainly couldn't have been expected to. It was then that he told me that there was no nurse – that Randi had refused to go to the hospital and after a huge argument, that it had been just them and a couple of her drugged out friends. He sobbed that he blamed himself and that he hated her for the fact that she wouldn't go to the hospital. I could tell that he hated himself more for not being able to make her go. We sat on those steps until the sun went down and although he stopped crying eventually, he wouldn't accept that it wasn't his fault.

Kev flatly refused to go back in to see Randi. He said he never wanted to see her again and that he wanted me to get her out of his house. I tried to feel sorry for her but I couldn't. I couldn't stop thinking that if she had stopped taking drugs or had gone to the hospital when she was supposed to, that none of this would have happened. I finally went inside but all I felt was disgust when I saw her sitting on the bed smoking a joint. I tried to be polite and asked her how she was feeling but she was so matter-of-fact I wanted to slap her. She was so intent on sucking on that joint she could barely answer me. I couldn't believe that she was more interested in getting stoned than the fact that her baby was dead, while Kev was outside in pieces over it. I yelled at her to get out and to take her stoner friends with her. Unbelievably, she told me to 'chill out' and that it wasn't that bad. I had never hit a girl before but I hit her then – I slapped her so hard her head snapped back. Then I grabbed her and dumped her on the floor like a rag doll. She jumped up and glared at me – sparks flying from her eyes. "How dare you touch me!" she screamed, "You will regret this!"

I took a menacing step towards her and she fled, her drugged out mates helping her stagger out. I heard the front door slam and a few heated words on the verandah and then she was gone.

I looked over at the bed where there was a blanket with a tiny hump in it. I walked over to it and picked it up. He was so tiny and didn't really look dead, just cold and a bit blue. I wrapped him tighter in the blanket and walked outside where I held him out to Kev. He turned and saw me, hesitating a second before reaching out and taking the baby in his arms. He stood, gazing down at the little face, tears splashing down. I had to turn away, I was so choked up. I think I was crying mostly for Kev and the little person who never had a chance. He never even lived and somehow he was dead – it just didn't seem fair. Somehow, together Kev and I cleaned up and arranged for an ambulance to take the body away. After everyone was gone, we sat in the house in silence. I didn't know what to say and he couldn't seem to think of any words either. After a few hours like that, I couldn't stand it any more and told him I had to go. He thanked me and said he couldn't have gotten through it without me. I just nodded and left – I had no words and no tears left in me.

In the end, there wasn't a big funeral or any fuss – Kev couldn't afford anything much and Randi didn't seem to care. There was an inquest and a state funded burial and the baby now lies in the Grace cemetery with only a cheap flat plaque to prove that he ever existed. I went out there once with Kev and it was almost more than he could take – the plot was only a tiny mound and the headstone was nondescript. No name, no nothing. I looked at Kev looking at that headstone and I could feel the weight of his sadness. He cried and said he couldn't do anything right – not even bury his son.

I saw Randi around town a few times in the months after wards and she seemed ok - acting as if nothing had even happened. Once when she was at the mall, laughing and joking with her friends, she saw me and Kev and backed off nervously. I spat on the ground near her and just walked away. If I ever speak to her again, it will be too soon. Kev started talking about cutting out – leaving town for a while. I wished he would – I thought he might go nuts if he had to walk around seeing Randi everywhere. And finally he did go out of town, said he was going to look for work up North for a while – get his head straight. Dave and I continued to hang out but it all felt changed and too quiet without Kev. Rumour around town was that Randi had started seeing our old enemy Wayne – all I could think was that she had sunk lower than ever.

Privately we thought it was all to do with getting back at Kev and we only hoped when he got back he would be past caring what she did.

It wasn't too long before we saw Wayne and Randi together outside the local shops. Wayne smirked at us and held out his hand like he wanted to shake, saying it had been too long and that we should start over. His mouth was smiling but his eyes were lying and Dave just spat on his outstretched hand. We told him we would have nothing to do with a low life scum like him or his skanky girlfriend. Wayne wiped his hand, shoved Dave hard and told him to watch his back. Randi just stood there the whole time – nervous but obviously proud of her tough-guy boyfriend. It was then that Wayne pulled out a butterfly knife and waved it in my face. He told me that I would pay for what I had said and done to Randi. So smooth and fast, he swiped that knife along my face, opening my cheek up. I tasted hot blood and it drove me wild. My head was full of nothing but bright, hot hate and I leapt at him, grabbing the knife by the blade. Later I needed stitches to sew up the deep cut to my palm, but I didn't feel it at all just then. I only wanted to kill him and no pain was going to stop me. I turned that knife around and soon had it by the handle, holding it to his throat. My breath was coming in ragged gasps and I could vaguely hear Dave yelling at me to stop but

I couldn't. I kicked Wayne in the balls and jumped on top of him as he fell, knife still at his throat. His eyes were bulging with fear and he must have thought he was surely going to die. I probably would have cut his throat then, had Randi not leapt on my back, clawing my face and pulling my hair. I flung her off and backhanded her across the face. I then walked over to where she fell and lay shrieking. I waved the knife in her face and she shut up pretty quick. I was honestly out of control – I was ready to kill and I didn't care if it was her or him or both of them. Dave grabbed my arm and bent it back, pinning the knife behind me. "That's enough man!" he shouted, "Lets just go, ok" He held me for a few seconds more and I regained enough sense to realise what I was about to do. I took a deep breath and nodded. Dave let me go and we got ready to leave. I couldn't resist giving Wayne a hard kick in the ribs as we left and spat on Randi and she lay there, still crying and screaming.

We ended up back at Dave's and thankfully his old man was out – I couldn't deal with any more hassle right then. We went to the bathroom and mopped the blood off my face and hand. The cut on my cheek wasn't too bad – probably could've used some stitches but I hated hospitals and figured it would heal soon enough on its own. The hand I wrapped in bandages but by midnight it was still bleeding and I was at the

emergency room getting them both sewn up. I couldn't
believe that Dave gave me a lecture – demanding to know
what I thought I was doing and telling me that the last thing
that Kev needed was for me to give him something else to feel
guilty about. I could see his point but just I hated her with a
passion that made me crazy and her being with that loser just
made it worse.

A few days after this, Kev came back into town – he had
chucked the job up North and was back home for now. We
thought it was better not to tell him what happened with
Wayne & Randi and I spun a story about my scars. He barely
raised an eyebrow at my outlandish claims – he seemed flat
and depressed. His whole manner seemed distracted and he
started spending all his time at the Rec again. We hardly saw
him for weeks on end. Rumour had it that he was dealing
again and even stranger, that he might have been doing
business for Wayne and his crew. I asked him about it on at
least two occasions but he was evasive and told me to stay
out of it. Needless to say, Dave and I were really worried
about him and what he had gotten into. He continued to avoid
us and soon it had been months since we had seen him.
Word on the street was that he was selling and worse - *using*
some heavy shit and had huge debts hanging over him. Word
on the street also had it that Wayne and his crew had fed him

drugs until he was hooked and now he was indebted to them for his habit and the money he owed them.

One night I decided to go over to his house and confront him. Dave really didn't want to go – big emotional scenes weren't his thing. He said I should go talk to Kev and that he would go and see what he could find out from Wayne and his crew. So at about 9 o'clock, I walked over to Kev's. I wasn't looking forward to this at all.

As I got closer to his house, I saw a lone figure sitting on the steps. When I got real close, I saw the shadowed eyes, the pale gaunt face and the needle tracks too. I couldn't believe my eyes. I called his name and he looked up at me with blurry, bloodshot eyes. I like to think I could still see some of the old Kev in his twisted face. He told me to sit down and I did. I tried to make conversation with him but he was just too out of it. He kept asking me where I had been and why I had left him alone so long. It was a really weird experience and when I felt I couldn't take anymore, I stood up to go. I was almost crying as I looked down at him. I yelled at him then, asking him why he was doing this and then I had to stop because I was really bawling. As I turned to walk away, he started to laugh. A sad, crazy twisted laugh that echoed in the night.

I walked for hours, going nowhere and thinking almost nothing. I was just shocked and tired and used up. I couldn't believe that Kev had gotten into this state and that we hadn't even known. Maybe the truth was, we hadn't wanted to know. I kept walking until I finally came back near Kev's and ran into Dave. I told him what had happened and how Kev had looked. Dave told me he would go back to Kev's and make sure he was ok. I trudged off down the street but was only at the corner when I heard Dave screaming my name. He raced up to me panting and hysterical. He managed to tell me that Kev was in bad shape. He said that he had gotten to the house and had seen Kev lying on the verandah. He hadn't answered when Dave called to him and when he got closer, he could see that his lips were blue and he wasn't breathing. Together we ran back to Kev's – he was still lying slumped over and not moving. I grabbed his arm and shook him. I slapped his face and I lifted his eyelids but nothing seemed to affect him. I tried to remember the first aid we had learned all those years ago in school but all I could recall was to check his pulse. There wasn't one. I screamed to Dave to call an ambulance and he ran inside to do so. I laid Kev down flat on the veranda and tried to remember how to do CPR. I blew into his mouth a few times but it didn't seem to do anything –

frantically I thumped his chest and kept breathing into his mouth.

The ambulance seemed to take hours but I know it was only minutes before they got there and seemed like only seconds before they said he was dead. Dave and I just stared at each other, stunned. Dead? Kev dead? No way – he was only just 18 years old and his life had only just started – how could he be dead? I couldn't cry, I couldn't do anything as they pulled the sheet over his face and took him away in the ambulance. I just stood there, but Dave turned and slammed his fist into the wall of the house again and again. He screamed and sobbed – his heart must have been breaking to see yet another person he loved die right in front of his eyes.

We sat there on Kev's verandah until the sun came up and Kev's mother came walking up the front path, her shift obviously over. She called out a cheery hello and asked us if we were waiting for Kev. I looked at Dave and Dave looked at me. How were we going to tell her that Kev wouldn't be coming home that day or ever? She continued up the steps to the house, holding the screen door open for us. Dave and I exchanged another look and followed her inside.

Kev's mum continued to chatter on as she put the kettle on and started to make us something to eat. Dave and I were at a loss about how to tell her what had happened. We sat at her kitchen table, heads down and silent until she eventually stopped talking and came over to us. She laid a hand on each of our shoulders and asked us what was wrong. In a voice that was broken and raw, Dave told her that Kev had overdosed. She just looked at us with eyes that were just like Kev's and I knew then that she had loved him a lot more than she let on, more than he ever knew. She started to sob and fell to the kitchen floor. I bent down to help her and Dave tapped my arm – he looked at me with a hard light in his eyes and said he was leaving. I asked him where he was going and he said, "I've got business to take care of". I told him not to do anything crazy – it wouldn't change anything. He just smiled and walked out.

I sat there with Kev's mum for an hour or so – she continued to cry and I kept holding her. Eventually I left and just walked. I must have walked aimlessly for hours because when I came out of the daze, it was mid-day and hot. Exhausted, I sat on the kerb and cried some more. I don't know how long I sat there but it wasn't long enough because it didn't bring Kev back.

The next thing I remember is the wail of an ambulance and a couple of cop cars racing past me. I got up and followed the sirens to the rec centre where there was a large group of people standing around. I pushed my way to the front and saw Wayne lying in a pool of blood with Dave standing over him, gun in hand.

"Dave!" I screamed.

He looked up at me with dazed and glittering eyes. "I shot him" he said.

"You better split man, the cops are here" I shouted.

Dave only stood there. "He had it coming – he killed Kev" he mumbled.

Just then Randi flung herself out of the crowd and knelt beside Wayne. She looked at him bleeding from a shot in his head and two in his chest. She mopped blood from his face with her hands and leant her face next to his. She then jumped up and leapt at Dave screaming, "Murderer!" Her hands left big bloody prints on Dave's chest. He held her back with one hand and pointed the gun at her with the other. His voice was flat and cold as he said, "Someone better get this crazy bitch off me or she's gonna die too." But no-one came forward.

I stepped up to face Dave, "Let her go man" I said.

Dave just stared at me, "I thought you hated her? Wouldn't you like to see her lying next to him?" He laughed and pushed Randi to the ground and aimed the gun at her head.

I screamed, "Dave! No! Kev wouldn't have wanted you to do this"

He spat bitterly, "Yeah well Kev's dead or did you forget?"

I stood in front of Dave so the gun was pointed at me not Randi. "Want to kill someone else Dave? Go on then! Kill me – go ahead"

Dave stood there and for a second I truly thought he might pull the trigger but then his face changed and he lowered the gun. Just then 5 cops with guns drawn stepped through the crowd. They aimed at Dave and told him to put the gun down. His eyes went wild as he tried to think of a way out but there was none and he eventually dropped the gun. They tackled him to the ground and took him away in handcuffs. The ambos then came for Wayne and also took Randi away.

The crowd started to disperse and I turned to leave, exhausted and nearly hysterical with grief. I was grabbed by the shoulder and spun around. It was Butch with a deadly look on his face. "This isn't over", he spat, "You will pay for this".

I was so tired, too tired to go on with this crap. I told him we were even – Kev was dead and Wayne was dead. I told him we should forget this stupid feud and get on with life. He looked at me in dumb fury and told me that it wouldn't be over until I was dead too. I just shook my head and sighed – there are some people you just can't reach. I walked away from him and headed to the police station. I guessed they would have some questions for me and I wanted to see Dave.

I was questioned for about an hour and then waited another few hours before they let me see Dave. He seemed calm and under control when I finally got to talk to him. The bad news was that he was going down for murder and they weren't going to give him bail. I asked him if he had talked to a lawyer and he said Legal Aid had given him a free attorney or something. Dave said he didn't care one way or another because he didn't need a lawyer to plead guilty. I just looked at him. "Cant you plead insanity or something?" I said, "You might be able to get off"

Dave shook his head, "I wasn't insane mate you know that, no more insane than I've always been. I knew what I was doing and why. I'm not going to lie about it. It would be an insult to Kev if I lied about that. Don't worry – I can do the time"

I was sure he was doing his tough guy act but I wasn't impressed – I was scared. I didn't think he realised just how serious this was and what kind of time he would do for murder.

Because he couldn't get bail, he was told he would be held in custody to wait for his trial. It didn't seem to faze him that this might be months away – all he cared about was going to Kev's funeral. He had used that free lawyer only to apply for a special leave to attend the funeral. Amazingly he was granted it. He would be allowed 2 hours, heavily guarded of course, to go to the service and then he would be taken back to his cell.

I honestly don't know how I spent the four days leading up to Kev's funeral. I slept rough in the park because I couldn't handle going to Kev's without him being there and I certainly couldn't go to Dave's now that he was in jail. I know I went back and forth to the jail to see Dave in lock-up and back to the park to sleep. I lost a lot of time just wandering and thinking.

The day of the funeral was clear and sunny – the day seemed too beautiful to put my best friend in the ground. There were only a handful of people at the service and only four at the very front (not counting cops). There was me and Dave, Mrs

Harris and a man I recognised as Kev's father. I had only seen him a few times in all the years I had known Kev and not at all in the last few, but the set of his shoulders and his blue eyes were very familiar to me. It struck me as weird that he would be at his son's death when he had hardly been at his life.

The service was held at the graveside and Dave was un-handcuffed only long enough to carry his side of the polished black box that held Kev. As soon as the coffin was set down, two uniformed cops leapt forward to put the cuffs back on him. Did they really think he was going to kill someone at the funeral?

Kev's mother sobbed silently through the whole thing as the minister droned on and on. I stepped forward to say a few words when he had finished but I couldn't find the right words inside to say what I felt so I just said that. I said. "I don't know how to say all the things that need to be said about Kev. He was a brother to us, he was the best of us and he didn't deserve to die like this. Kev we miss you, we love you man." The last bit was said in a choked whisper as the tears flowed down my face. The coffin was lowered and that was that. It seemed so final, so much the end for all of us.

I left pretty much straight away and headed back to the park. I sat down and then noticed that Kev's old man had followed me. He sat down beside me and I just looked at him. He looked nervously away and cleared his throat.

"I just wanted to tell you how sorry I am about what happened", he said.

My voice was flat as I answered, "Shouldn't I be saying that to you?"

"Well, yes usually. But I know that you guys were closer than I have ever been to him and I know you must be hurting."

I looked at him with scorn, "Yeah. So. What do you want?"

"Nothing really. I just wanted to tell you that I thought he was a hell of a kid. Even though I didn't see him that much, I never stopped caring for him."

I interrupted rudely then, "Yeah well, it's a bit late for that now isn't it? Is that going to make up for all the years he thought it was his fault you never came around? Is that going to mean his mother wouldn't have to work 2 jobs and he wouldn't have to deal drugs because you never gave them a cent? Is it going to make him be alive again? Just save it ok – I don't buy it and I don't want to hear it right now."

Kev's dad at least had the decency to look ashamed but that only made me feel like an asshole.

"Look man" I said, "I'm sorry, but I just can't do this right now, you know?"

"Yeah ok. Ok. I came up here because Kev's mum thought you could come over and go through Kev's things for her. She isn't up to it and I don't feel right doing it. You don't have to - it's up to you."

"Allright, I'll come over later ok?"

"Why don't you come now?" He said. "We can walk back together." The way he said it, it sounded like a command not a question so I got up and followed him.

When we got to Kev's house, I could see why he had wanted me to come straight away. Kev's mum had packed everything from the rest of the house into boxes. The only room she hadn't touched was Kev's. "I just couldn't do it" she said, "Thanks for coming". I nodded and went into his room. The whole room was just pure Kev. The walls were covered in posters – cars, bikes and women of course but a whole wall was covered in pictures of baby seals. It was this contrast that summed up his personality.

His bed was unmade and the floor was littered with clothes and junk but yet his desk was immaculate, with a typewriter and stacks of typed pages in piles. I tried to open the desk drawer but it was locked so I jimmied the lock with my knife.

There was only one thing in the drawer; a bulging black file thick with paper.

I felt a little weird reading what was in there because he had kept it locked up and all, but I did it anyway. Most of it was poetry he had clipped out of books and magazines but a few were ones he had written himself. Some I remembered from the times he had read them to us, but the recent ones were different. They were dark and full of depression and pain. I never knew Kev had so much hurt inside him. I thought I knew him so well. I sat there reading for an hour or more and one of the poems stuck in my head like an infected splinter;

well…

so what…

i deserve to die

never did anything

was never going to be anything

better off dead

been dead a while anyway

but alive

in a way

walking

talking

breathing

but nothing left inside

empty heart

empty mind

no-one cares

no-one to cry

if i

end it all

end it now...

It was dated the same night he had died. I read that and just broke down. I never knew he felt like this, he never talked about it. I guess he kept it all inside until it tangled up and choked him. It made me too sad to think that he might not have known what he meant to us. It devastated me to think he may have intentionally overdosed that night.

I ended up spending the rest of that day in Kev's room and when I left I only had the black file in my hand. I had packed up everything else into boxes and carried them into the front room. Kev's mum was just sitting there staring at nothing. It seemed like she had been like that for hours. I asked her if she was ok and she looked at me with hate in her eyes, "My son just died a stupid, senseless, dirty death. I am not ok. No. I'm not ok." I could tell that she wished it had been me who had died – not just me, anyone but Kev. I sat down beside her and held out the book of poems. She looked at them in silence, with tears rolling down her face.

"I had no idea" she sobbed, "I should have known. Why didn't I see?"

I tried to comfort her by saying that no-one knew, no-one could have saved him. But I didn't believe that and she knew it too. I knew we were all to blame. But at the same time, part of me felt that if he was in that much pain when he was alive, maybe he was at least at peace now. Kev's mum let me take the poems and I left with a heavy heart. That was the last time I ever saw her or the inside of that house. I walked by it many times afterwards but it was nothing but an empty shell without Kev.

The months leading up to Dave's trial were a blur. I found a job labouring with the council and rented a small room at a boarding house. I was working and saving hard and spending whatever spare time I had with Dave at the lock up. He was still intent on pleading guilty and no matter what I said I couldn't talk him out of it. His lawyer was equally frustrated and knew that the guilty plea was a one way ticket to a long jail term.

The day of the trial, the court was packed with friends of ours and friends of Wayne. I saw that Butch and Randi were seated at the front, waiting expectantly. The lawyer had told us that the trial wouldn't last long due to the guilty plea but that the judge had indicated that he wanted to hear Dave's story in order to get a clear picture of what had happened and why. So, after the lawyer had entered the plea, Dave went up to the stand to explain what happened. He sat there straight and proud, face grim and determined. The judge asked him a few questions about the ongoing feud and about Kev and about the previous fights we had had with Wayne and his crew. Dave answered every question straight up and honest, even though his lawyer winced every time he did. He was clearly making a noose for himself but he didn't seem to care. Even when the judge asked him if he had any remorse for what he had done, Dave would not lie. Dave just said that the only thing he was sorry about was that Kev was dead. The judge then asked him about his 'state of mind' at the time of the shooting and Dave said the worst thing he probably could have.

"I'm not crazy if that's what you mean" he said, "not then and not now. I knew what I was doing and why I did it. In fact, I would do it again today." The judge just shook his head and dismissed him from the stand.

The judge told everyone to have a break and that he would sentence Dave after lunch. I walked over to him, furious and scared. "Do you have any idea what you just did" I demanded.

He looked me straight in the eyes and said, "Yeah man. I took the rap for what I did. I did it for Kev. I told you how it was going to be".

I just stared at him in disbelief. I knew there was no point in arguing with him now.

"Any idea what kind of time you are looking at?" I finally asked.

He smiled wryly, "Yeah, the lawyer said they're talking about 15-20 years. Lucky we don't have the death penalty here hay?"

I tried to smile back but I was sick inside to think of him spending 15-20 years locked up.

Eventually the judge came back and everyone sat, ready to hear the sentence. It really pissed me off to hear the things he said before announcing the sentence. He said Dave was a disgrace and a danger to society, that he was possibly even a sociopath! He said Dave had shown no remorse and could not expect to be rehabilitated as he appeared to have no conscience and no sense of right and wrong. I knew that the judge was only seeing the outside of Dave and that he had no way of knowing the real Dave but it was really frustrating to sit there and listen to that. He finally got to the end of his speech and sentenced Dave to 18 years in maximum security. He said he would not be making Dave eligible for parole. The court was in an uproar after that – Butch and his buddies actually clapped and cheered, while our friends were furious. I looked towards Dave and saw that he wore a small smile. I shook my head in disbelief – I wanted to think he was crazy but I knew he wasn't. He was confused, hurt, angry and cynical but not crazy. It came to me in that instant that maybe he was as screwed up and suicidal as Kev had been.

I left the court in a daze. I couldn't comprehend that I had lost another friend. I was really alone now. As I stumbled from the building, I came face to face with Butch and two of his mates. He made some stupid comment about there being 'two down and one to go'. I tried to side step him and walk away but he got right in my face and said he was serious and that I should know that I was going down next. I felt nothing but cold hard anger in my heart. I wanted to pull out my knife and stick it in his chest but I just pushed him away and told him to back off. He kept on taunting me, right up in my face and not backing off. Eventually I snapped and ripped my blade out of my back pocket, flicking it open. I told him in no uncertain terms that if he messed with me again, I would bury him. He must have seen the truth in my words because he stepped back and let me pass.

I left then and went to the jail to wait for visiting hours. I spent that hour talking to Dave, telling him that I was leaving this place, getting out. I told him I was sorry I wouldn't be there to visit him but that I would write and phone but that I had to go. I knew he understood, maybe him going to jail was his way of getting out too. We talked and laughed and cried until the visiting time was up. Then I went to my little room and packed my things, grabbed the money I had saved from working all those months and went to the station. I got on the first Greyhound out of there.

Again, the months passed like days and I found it harder and harder to write or phone Dave but I kept doing it because I knew I was all he had. I had put away the flannel, gotten a hair cut and a job and tried to bury myself in my new life.

Each day it got easier for me to breathe and to think about Kev and Dave without breaking down. I still felt the pain and the ghosts still lived in my head but with the help of a counsellor I started to accept it and the wounds had started to heal. I finally started to think that maybe I could see a future for myself out of the neighbourhood and out of all the shit.

I kept working and saving and trying to make new friends. I was having a hard time with that and the counsellor told me I was afraid to get close to people. I told her that everyone I had ever got close to had left me. She said I couldn't let that stop me. I told her that was easier said than done. She told me that people don't leave you if you keep them in your heart. I told her I didn't want them in my heart, I wanted them here in front of me. Often our conversations went this way – she made it seem so simple to move on and start afresh but I knew it was a long hard road.

It was after one of these sessions and just when the road was starting to look shorter that it all hit home to me again. I was feeling ok and had stopped to grab the paper to read in the park, like old times. The name of my hometown jumped up at me and I read about a riot at the jail. Dozens hurt and one inmate had been trampled to death. I was sick with dread as I looked over the story and sure enough, there was his name.

My first instinct was to curl up and die myself. Now everyone I loved was dead. I truly was alone.

What followed that day were some of the darkest days I had ever been through. I wasn't sleeping or eating and one night I found myself with an empty bottle of Jacks and a handful of pills. I woke up in the hospital – my counsellor had come around after I missed my session – she found me and called the ambulance. Having my stomach pumped and lying there sick as a dog in that sterile place gave me a reality check. I won't act like I saw any white light or heard any bullshit angels calling me – but a straight talking doctor made me realise how pathetic it would be for me to take my own life. He told me that nobody actually cared if I lived or died and that I would just be another statistic if I didn't get my shit together. That really pissed me off and when I tried to grab him from the bed, he laughed and said he knew I wasn't ready to die. He told me my spirit was strong and I was destined for better things. I told him I didn't dig that bullshit hippy talk and I turned my back to him. But I did realise I had to go on – after all I had been through it would be too easy to die. I didn't want to be just another loser from the hood who met a predictable end. I wanted to make the lives of Kev, Dave (and me) actually matter.

Later when my counsellor came in, I started asking her about me maybe going back to school. Maybe I could do something to help other 'bogans' 'bums' and 'losers' – other kids from the streets who cant see any future that doesn't include drugs and guns and jail. She thought that was a great idea and said I would be the perfect role model. I told her that she and the doc should get together with their fancy talking – all I wanted to do was help screwed up kids get on the straight and narrow. She said that a man who had been through a fire and could show his scars would be the perfect person to teach kids not to play with matches. I told her I been shot at, stabbed, beaten and battered but I ain't never been burned. She just laughed and called me unique. Well that's one name I never been called before...

Truckin'.

He had been standing in the same spot, just past the intersection, for over an hour trying to catch a ride. It was 4am and no-one would stop. Maybe it was the approaching dawn or the fat rain drops that had started to fall. More likely, people just did not like the look of him. He had been on the road for a long time and it was days between showers and meals – he couldn't even remember the last time he had shaved. Add to that the fire that blazed inside him and caused his eyes to glow almost red with madness – little wonder no-one would stop.

So he just stood there, thumb out and watched the cars roll past. A few trucks went by and although he had always had better luck with the big rigs, tonight they kept cruising past. Finally he had had enough – he was cold and hungry and dog tired. He looked up and saw a big semi slowly rolling through the lights. He stepped out into the road and sprung like a tiger up onto the bull bar where he clung tight as the truck kept going. He inched his way up so his face was level with the windscreen and smiled in at the driver. He was somewhat surprised to see that the driver was a young girl – had to be 19 years old tops. She stared back at him – more anger than fear on her face as she started hollering at him. He just kept on smiling his empty grin and began to inch his way around to the passenger door.

The driver blew the airhorn and put her foot down hard – obviously trying to dislodge him. The fury on her face told him that she would most likely run those big wheels right over him if he did fall.

But he did not fall. He had reached the far side of the wrap-around bull bar and stretched his long spidery arm out to open the door. Of course the door swung open into him and he was ready for this. He quickly switched his leech-like grip from the bull bar to the door and swung his body around the door, for an instant fluttering in mid air, only tethered by his hands. He then flung his body forward into the gap and landed dead centre in the passenger seat. The door slammed shut seconds afterwards. It was not the first time he had done this.

He looked over at the girl driver and smiled. His sharp incisors and missing molars were obvious. "Thanks for the ride" he drawled, "Been standin' there a fair while"

She glared back at him and began to down-shift the huge rig – clearly intending to stop and force him out.

"I aint takin' you nowhere mister – I ride alone", she spat.

He kept on smiling and reached into his jacket where he kept his blade. He took it out and toyed with it idly, looking up at her with hooded eyes.

"Oh I think you could use some company tonight, don't you?", he whispered slyly.

She glanced over at the knife and directly up into his eyes. She spoke flatly;

"I aint scared of you or your stupid knife. This is my rig and I say who rides and who don't ride"

In an instant he had the blade at her throat. "Well baby girl, tonight I say who rides"

She put the truck back into gear and let the speed build back up. She ignored the knife at her throat and spoke calmly.

"Well I was planning on stopping soon – I need to eat and rest. So I can only take you a little ways up the road."

He grinned wolfishly and slid the blade back into his pocket.

"I'm real glad we could come to an agreement, doll" he said, "I could use a break myself – where you planning on bunking down?"

She gestured over her shoulder towards a darkened sleeping compartment behind the cab, "I sleep in there. You can find your own bed for the night"

He chuckled, "You a tough cookie are ya honey?"

She rolled her eyes and kept on driving.

They drove on in silence for about an hour. Neither spoke or moved. The hitchhiker looked at her out of the corners of his snake eyes but she didn't once turn her head.

She finally slowed the big rig and turned down a short gravel lane into a rest stop. She looked over at the man next to her and spoke slowly and clearly;

"Looks like this is where you get out cowboy. You should be able to get another ride here fairly soon"

He yawned and stretched elaborately. "You know what baby girl – I think I'm going to stay put. I can just snuggle up with you back there."

She glared at him furiously, "I don't think so mister! This is where you get out."

He stared back at her lazily. "Naw, I don't think so"

"Look mister – I gave you a ride, now you need to get out of my truck."

He just kept on grinning. The look in his eyes un-settled her and she broke the stare first.

It was a tough situation – venomous snake versus broken doll. At the same time they reached down, each coming up with their weapon of choice. He had his trusty blade and she, a snub nosed pistol, kept down the side of the seat for just this sort of occurrence. They both leveled the weapons at each other and glared into each other's eyes.

It was a Mexican standoff. Neither would admit defeat and neither would weaken or lower their weapon. Time stood still and almost half an hour passed with no movement from either of them. A burst of static emitting from the two-way radio finally broke them out of their trance and, startled, they both laughed. After that it seemed easy to put down the weapons and share a lukewarm drink from the thermos she had in back.

Eventually, sharing the drink led to chat and they discovered that they had more in common than they first thought. After all, a sociopath is only two steps removed from the victim and each had been both in many ways. She had been violated by her father and reacted badly after years of torture, when caught running away from home she had put 6 bullets into his brain. He had killed his own father for violating him and his sister, slicing his throat and watching until he bled out.

She had tried to run from the horror and he had only thought to stop the horror but both had been cast out for their actions. She had been accused of seduction, deceitfulness and failure to conform to the authority of her father. He had been accused of lack of remorse and anti-social behaviour.

Both had since roamed the country alone and broken. At times they had both committed acts that went against God and nature. Both had taken the philosophy 'kill or be killed' and used it to survive.

The long night of talk led to a partnership cemented in shared experience. He no longer had to travel the lonely highway on his own and she could finally stop driving long roads to nowhere. Within each defective person, there lay the ingredients for one whole strong person. Together they could roam the country and lay waste to useless ghosts of the past. God help anyone who got in their way.

end.

www.ingramcontent.com/pod-product-compliance
Lightning Source LLC
Chambersburg PA
CBHW060421260626
47161CB00005B/1727